Presented To:

_____

From:

_____

Date:

_____

WILL
TO WIN

OTHER DESTINY IMAGE BOOKS AND MOVIES BY JIM STOVALL

The Ultimate Gift

The Ultimate Life

The Ultimate Journey

The Ultimate Legacy

The Millionaire Map

The Ultimate Financial Plan

Ultimate Hindsight

The Gift of a Legacy

A Christmas Snow

Success Secrets of Super Achievers

Today's the Day!

The Art of Learning and Self-Development

The Art of Productivity

The Art of Presentation

The Art of Communication

The Financial Crossroads

Ultimate Productivity

Keeper of the Flame

The Lamp

Poems, Quotes, and Things to Think About

Wisdom of the Ages

Discovering Joye

Top of the Hill

One Season of Hope

Wisdom for Winners Volume 1, 2, 3, 4

100 Worst Employees

WILL
TO WIN

A Tale of Humor
and Perspective from
Will Rogers High School

JIM STOVALL

Published and distributed by:
SOUND WISDOM
P.O. Box 310
Shippensburg, PA 17257-0310
717-530-2122
info@soundwisdom.com
www.soundwisdom.com

Cover/jacket designer Eileen Rockwell
Interior design by Terry Clifton

ISBN 13 TP: 978-1-64095-179-2
ISBN 13 HC: 978-1-64095-172-3
ISBN 13 eBook: 978-1-64095-173-0

For Worldwide Distribution, Printed in the U.S.A.
1 2 3 4 5 6 7 8 / 23 22 21 20

Look into the depths

Of another's soul
And listen,
Not only with our ears,
But with our hearts
And imagination
And our silent love.

BY JOYE KANELAKOS

As quoted in *The Ultimate Gift* by Jim Stovall

CONTENTS

Foreword *by Steve Gragert* 1

Introduction *by Jim Stovall* 5

Chapter One   An Ancient People 11

Chapter Two   Where Two Worlds Collide 21

Chapter Three   Out on a Limb .31

Chapter Four   Trial by Fire 39

Chapter Five   A Moment of Truth 49

Chapter Six   Restoration and Renewal 57

Chapter Seven   Past, Present, and Future 65

Chapter Eight   Work and Play 73

Chapter Nine   Leaders and Politicians 81

Chapter Ten   Point of No Return 93

Chapter Eleven   In the Spotlight 103

Chapter Twelve   Going to the Source 115

Chapter Thirteen   Enemy Territory 125

Chapter Fourteen   Into the Fire 135

Chapter Fifteen   Going to the Well 145

Chapter Sixteen   End of the Trail 153

Chapter Seventeen A New Path 167

About the Author 177

FOREWORD

by Steve Gragert

In *Will to Win,* best-selling author Jim Stovall continues his highly acclaimed and inspiring *Homecoming Historical Series.* His newest offering is an uplifting, emotional, and enlightening story of Sky Forest, a senior at an Oklahoma high school that bears the name of Will Rogers, the undisputed favorite son of young Sky's state of birth and of the Cherokee people, his and her own blood and cultural heritage.

Readers will experience the lows and highs of Sky's last year as an aspiring athlete at Will Rogers, the extreme range of disappointments and successes she has to face and overcome, with the words and perceived presence of Will Rogers and the Cherokee wisdom of her grandmother reinforcing her will and determination to beat the odds and to "win."

Having been fortunate to spend my professional life researching, studying, and sharing the life, words, and wisdom of Will Rogers, I have always been pleased to experience another writer's contributions to the world of Will. With *Will to Win* Jim Stovall has created and crafted a unique, entertaining, and inspiring story that, I believe, Will would heartily applaud, by no means because of the mentions of him in it, but rather because of its baseball-centered storyline—his favorite sport—and the story's keen communication of Cherokee traditions and beliefs. Most significantly, he would endorse the positive values it lifts up. He would view Sky and her story as fitting well his ultimate measurement of the quality of a life that he expressed in one of his writings: "It's great to be great but it's greater to be human."

The same can be said of Jim, his life and his accomplishments. Enjoy this latest work of Jim Stovall. Each of us can learn much from the *Will to Win*.

STEVE GRAGERT
Executive Director, Retired
Will Rogers Memorial Museums

INTRODUCTION

by Jim Stovall

My Dear Reader,

I want to thank you for the investment of time and money you have made in this book. I have written more than forty books with millions of copies in print, and I remain grateful for every person who picks up one of my titles and takes a journey with me. To date, eight of my books have been turned into movies, and this story has already been optioned for the big screen.

As with all my books, *Will to Win* is designed to be entertaining, informative, and help you change the course of your life.

This is the third novel in my *Homecoming Historical* series with more to follow. *One Season of Hope* dealt with the life and legacy of Harry S. Truman and a group of special fictitious young people at Truman High. *Top of the Hill* dealt with the life and legacy of Napoleon Hill in much the same way. Within these pages, you and I will visit a fictitious Will Rogers High School, meet some amazing young people, and explore the wit, wisdom, and worldwide timeless impact of Will Rogers.

None of my more than forty books, including this one, would have been possible without the tireless efforts and patience of my treasured colleague and friend Dorothy Thompson.

I want to thank Steve Gragert for writing the Foreword to this book and for providing his valuable expertise as one of the foremost historians on the life of Will Rogers. I want to thank Jennifer Rogers-Etcheverry, Will's great granddaughter, for her support of this story in print as well as on the movie screen. I want to thank

Russ Kirkpatrick and Andy Kinslow, the executive producers of the *Will to Win* movie, for believing in this story and the potential of the message.

I am grateful for having had the privilege of interviewing the late Doris "Coke" Meyer, Will Rogers' niece and author of the book *I Called Him Uncle Will*. When I interviewed her in 2012, she was 95 years old and the last living relative who knew Will Rogers personally. She told me of her time with Will Rogers in Beverly Hills, California, when he seemed like a celebrity and a superstar, and she spoke of her time with him in Oklahoma where he seemed like a common man, a good neighbor, and a friend to all.

I grew up loving the game of baseball. My father played semi-pro ball and has the distinction of having played in a game with the legendary Mickey Mantle. It has been exciting to rekindle my love of the game within these pages.

I want to thank Sarah Hudek for her willingness to share her baseball career and life experiences in an interview with me. Sarah is a real-life example of the path taken by the main character of this story.

I owe a great debt to the dedicated professionals at the Will Rogers Memorial Museum, and I am grateful to generous and learned individuals within the Cherokee Nation for their help in allowing me to provide a small glimpse into their past, present, and future.

As you get involved with this story and experience the lives of its characters, I hope you will think of your own goals and dreams, and renew your commitment to living your best possible life.

Any time I can be of encouragement or assistance to you on your path to greatness, I can be reached at Jim@JimStovall.com.

You were born with a dream to win and the talent to win. Now I hope you will find the will to win.

JIM STOVALL

2018

Chapter One

An Ancient People

"We are just here for a spell and pass on...so get a few laughs, do the best you can.... Live your life so that whenever you lose, you are ahead."
—WILL ROGERS

1

The old woman stared into the fire just as countless numbers of her people had done since the beginning of time. On clear nights, she was fond of gazing up into the heavens and imagining each of the myriad of flickering stars as campfires surrounded by her ancestors.

The glow from the flames that shone on her face revealed the many wrinkles etched into her skin. It appeared like a map showing the ancient trails traveled by her tribe. The trails of the Cherokee people had led through victory, defeat, joy, and tears.

She was proud to be a Cherokee woman. She knew that other women did not hold the place of honor and respect that Cherokee women held. Her people were matrilineal, which meant that Cherokees established their lineage through women. Each generation was counted from mother to daughter. The Cherokee people were also matrilocal, which meant that, unlike other civilizations, in the Cherokee tradition when a man married a woman, he would live with or close to her family. Cherokee women were part of the creation process and represented the past, the present, and the future.

The fire gave Matilda Forest warmth, comfort, and a sense of belonging that it had always given to her people. She considered how, once a fire was started, it could be used to light many fires without being diminished. There was enough fire for everyone and everything.

Matilda was startled by an unexpected sound behind her. She turned away from the brick fireplace and saw her granddaughter, Sky Forest, coming in the front door of their modern suburban home. Matilda looked lovingly at her granddaughter who was tall, strong, and graceful. Her beauty and proud bearing would be the envy of any 17-year-old girl.

Matilda was struck by the fact that her granddaughter was becoming more of a young woman than a girl with each passing day, but on this day, she could read Sky's frustration and disappointment on her young face just as she had been able to do since her granddaughter came to live with her as a small child.

It was hard to comprehend that the horrific car wreck that had instantly killed Sky's parents had been almost sixteen years before. In a heartbeat, Matilda's daughter and son-in-law were gone, but when the policeman handed Matilda her granddaughter wrapped in a blanket on that terrible night, she knew that, somehow, the best part of her daughter lived within her granddaughter, and her family would endure.

No one could ever explain how Sky had survived the wreck that took her parents. Everyone called it a miracle, but Matilda just thought of it as the heartbeat of her people living on.

Sky blurted, "Gram, it's the worst day ever," as she threw herself onto the sofa and slouched into the cushions.

Matilda settled into an armchair near the sofa and just gazed patiently at her granddaughter, knowing that the whole story would come out in good time. Patience comes easily to people who have lived through nearly 80 years, and Matilda had found her patience to be a powerful tool in leading, guiding, and raising her granddaughter.

As the tears began to roll down Sky's cheeks, she wailed, "It's all over!"

Matilda nodded sympathetically and waited for the full explanation she knew would be coming. She couldn't help but notice Sky was wearing her high school softball uniform. She was the star pitcher for the Will Rogers Ropers. Will Rogers' international fame had grown out of his skill in doing rope tricks, so the high school team name, Ropers, was a fitting tribute.

Matilda knew the first preseason workouts for the softball team had been scheduled for that afternoon, an event Sky had been anticipating for months as it was her senior year, and she was looking forward to finishing her high school softball career with a great season.

As Sky continued to cry uncontrollably, Matilda looked past her granddaughter at the dream catcher that hung on the wall of their living room. It was nearly two feet across and was decorated with rabbit fur and crystal beads. Matilda had always believed that dreams were coming toward us, past us, and around us every day. To her, the dream catcher had always been a reminder from her ancestors that we can focus on our greatest dreams and catch them before they slip away.

Most of the dreams Matilda had for her own life had already come true. She had married a wonderful man, and they had enjoyed a good life together until he passed away in his sleep a few years before. Her dreams had lived on through her daughter until they were all swept away in that fateful car crash, but now Matilda's remaining dreams, hopes, and ambitions lived in her granddaughter, Sky.

Eventually, Sky got her crying under control and spoke. "They've cancelled the softball season, and they're getting rid of the team. It's some kind of budget cutback."

Matilda prompted her granddaughter, "Tell me about it."

Sky drew in a ragged breath and continued. "We all showed up for the first day of softball practice, and everyone was really excited, but then the coach came in with the principal and some guy from the school board, and they told us it was all over."

Matilda's heart sank as she knew being the star pitcher on the Will Rogers High School softball team had been a big part of Sky's identity, self-esteem, and confidence.

Matilda asked, "How did everyone take the bad news?"

Sky's words were painful for her grandmother to hear.

"Well, everyone was disappointed, but they all have other things. Crystal has her cheerleading, Kelly has her music, and Brandi has her modeling; but softball was all I had."

Matilda wanted to tell her granddaughter that she was a lot more than a softball player, and her life would go on, but she knew it wasn't the time for those kinds of ideas just yet.

Sky concluded, "There's nothing left to do. We're just supposed to show up after school tomorrow and turn in our uniforms, and that's the end of it."

Matilda eased onto the couch next to her granddaughter and hugged her tightly. After a few moments, Sky stood up and wordlessly trudged down the hall to her bedroom and closed the door behind her.

Matilda prepared Sky's favorite dinner including cheeseburgers, French fries, and homemade apple pie. She usually tried to serve healthy and nutritious meals, but given the bad news and her granddaughter's emotional state, she was certain that cheeseburgers were in order. When everything was ready and she had the table set, Matilda walked down the hall to Sky's bedroom and tapped on the door.

She couldn't understand the mumbled response, so Matilda opened the door and announced,

"Dinner's ready."

Sky was lying face down across her bed and muttered, "I'm not hungry."

Matilda countered, "It's cheeseburgers, French fries, and apple pie."

Matilda turned and walked to the dining room table and sat down at her place knowing that Sky wouldn't be far behind. The dinner menu did its magic, and Sky appeared still wearing her softball uniform and slumped into her chair at the table.

The two ate in silence until Matilda offered, "There's something I'd like you to think about."

Sky looked up from her plate and grumbled, "This isn't going to be one of your Cherokee pep talks is it?"

Matilda just smiled as Sky continued.

"Gram, I know you're proud that we're Cherokee, and I know that can be a good thing, but that's not the world I live in when I'm at high school, and I'm not sure your Cherokee wisdom is going to have anything to do with my problem."

Matilda collected her thoughts, sighed briefly, and explained, "I love you, and wisdom is wisdom wherever it may come from, and unless you have a solution to your problem or some thoughts about it, maybe you should listen to what I have to say."

Sky nodded in resignation and continued to eat her French fries.

Matilda reached over and patted her granddaughter's arm, saying, "Sky, I know you're sad, frustrated, and angry, but you can't allow yourself to stay in that place."

Sky shrugged and asked, "Why not?"

Her grandmother explained, "There is a story about an old Cherokee chief who was teaching his grandson about life. 'A fight is going on inside me,' he said to the boy. 'It is a terrible fight, and it is between two wolves. One is evil. He is anger, envy, sorrow, regret, greed, arrogance, self-pity, guilt, resentment, inferiority, lies, false pride, superiority, self-doubt, and ego. The other is good. He is joy, peace, love, hope, serenity, humility, kindness, benevolence, empathy, generosity, truth, compassion, and faith. The same fight is going on inside you—and inside every other person, too.'

"The grandson thought about it for a minute and then asked his grandfather, 'Which wolf will win?'

"The old chief simply replied, 'The one you feed.'"

Matilda leaned back in her chair and waited for her granddaughter's reaction.

Sky rolled her eyes, sighed, and said with mock patience, "Gram, that's what you always do. When I have a real-world problem, you try to give me a Cherokee-world answer."

Matilda responded patiently, "The Cherokee world is the real world. You are Cherokee, and I am Cherokee, so the answers to our problems are Cherokee."

Sky shot back, "My problem is at Will Rogers High School."

Matilda smiled knowingly and pointed to the framed family heirloom hung on the dining room wall. It was an old black and white photograph of Will Rogers that he had signed and given to Matilda's father. Will had written: *Keep smiling. Will Rogers.*

Matilda explained, "Will Rogers was a Cherokee Indian and among the most famous and successful people of his time. He was proud of his success around the world and remained proud of his heritage in the Cherokee world. My father told me, 'Will Rogers took the best of being a Cherokee and the best of being an American and made the whole world a better place.'"

Matilda's heart soared as she saw the faintest hint of a smile on her granddaughter's face.

Sky declared, "Okay. I get it. But that's not easy."

Matilda solemnly stated, "Granddaughter, the best things in this life are never easy. They're simply the best things; and regardless of how you feel tonight, tomorrow is another day which might just bring you an unexpected solution to your problem."

Chapter Two

WHERE TWO WORLDS COLLIDE

*"They sent the Indians to Oklahoma. They
had a treaty that said, 'You shall have this
land as long as grass grows and water flows.'
It was not only a good rhyme but looked like
a good treaty, and it was till they struck oil."*
—WILL ROGERS

2

Matilda Forest followed her habit of rising early that next morning so she could enjoy the sunrise and greet the new day. As she sat on the deck behind her house, the sky in the east began to glow with promise. Matilda noted that spring was coming early that year in Tulsa, Oklahoma. She loved the hills and trees throughout the area especially when they displayed the bright green leaves of a new year. Tulsa was a beautiful city, and it was only about an hour's drive to the capital of the Cherokee Nation located in Tahlequah, Oklahoma.

As was her habit, Matilda began the day with a Cherokee prayer. "Oh, Great Spirit, help me always to speak the truth quietly, to listen with an open mind when others speak, and to remember the peace that may be found in silence."

Sky was usually bright and cheery in the morning, but that particular day, she was filled with gloom and despair.

As she shuffled into the kitchen for breakfast, her grandmother exclaimed, "Well, good morning to you, granddaughter."

Sky grunted unintelligibly and thrust her wadded-up softball uniform into a wrinkled grocery sack she found under the sink. Sky picked at her breakfast and left most of it uneaten.

Since Will Rogers High School was only a few blocks from the home where she and her grandmother lived, Sky enjoyed walking to school when the weather was nice. Her grandmother drove her to school when the weather was bad, or sometimes she loaned Sky the car.

Experiencing the fresh air and sunshine in the morning before classes began was always something Sky looked forward to except for that day when she walked aimlessly through the neighborhood clutching the rumpled grocery sack containing her softball uniform. Her Will Rogers High School softball uniform had always been an object of pride and joy for her, but now it seemed like a burst balloon or an empty promise. She could not have imagined having to turn in her uniform on a gorgeous spring day in her senior year before the softball season had even begun.

Will Rogers High School had been built in 1939, only four years after its namesake's tragic death in a plane crash. The school became known as "Will on the Hill" and was added to the National Register of Historic Places. The U.S. Park Service proclaimed Will Rogers High School in Tulsa, Oklahoma, to be one of the great examples of Art Deco architecture.

Many celebrities and notable figures have graduated from Will Rogers High School in Tulsa, Oklahoma, including professional athletes, entertainers, politicians, and business leaders. The school had grown over the years to a point where it sprawled over twenty-six acres east of downtown Tulsa.

None of this was on Sky Forest's mind as she walked through the front door of her high school that fateful day.

Since her first day of class, Sky had always paused each day by the statue of Will Rogers in the lobby of the school. On most days, she could almost swear that Will was looking down at her or even winking at her as if he had something to say. The base of the statue was inscribed with the words most connected to Will Rogers: *"I never met a man I didn't like."*

On that morning, Sky thought that old Will never met the guy from the school board who cut the budget and cancelled her softball team. She couldn't imagine even Will Rogers liking him.

Sky sleepwalked in a daze through her classes that day, and just before the last period, she went back to her locker, got out the grocery bag containing her softball uniform, and trudged toward the locker room to give back the last vestige of her dream.

It was over without any fanfare or ceremony. One of the equipment managers took Sky's softball uniform from her and crossed her name off a list he had on a clipboard.

Her heart was heavy as Sky walked aimlessly down the hall toward the front door of the school. She took no notice of the statue of Will Rogers, but just as she was approaching the outer door, she thought she heard a voice say, "Go to the softball field one more time."

Sky whirled around to see who had spoken, but there was no one around her except the bronze statue of Will Rogers that seemed to be looking directly at her with a knowing smile on his face. Sky stood in shocked silence for several moments, then shrugged and said, "Why not?"

She bounded out the front door into the gorgeous afternoon. The sun shone brightly, the birds sang cheerily, and Sky could hear the familiar sound of a bat hitting a ball as she approached the softball field. For just a moment, her hopes soared; but then as she rounded the corner, she noticed that some of the high school baseball players were working out on the softball field.

She asked one of the younger players unloading bags of equipment, "What's going on?"

He looked up and noticed Sky standing there and seemed unable to speak for a moment. Sky couldn't help but think how ridiculous guys had been acting around her for the last year or so, but she shrugged it off as one of life's imponderables, remaining totally oblivious to the impact her grace and regal beauty had on her male counterparts.

Finally, the young man was able to collect himself and stammer, "Well, it's just an informal preseason workout before tryouts for pitchers on Monday."

Sky turned to walk home but paused when she heard a voice say, "Why don't you sit down, and watch for a while?"

She turned back toward the young man unloading equipment and asked, "Did you say something?"

He was so startled, he stepped on a bat and nearly fell down. His voice cracked as he said, "No, I didn't say anything."

Sky was bewildered but thought, *Why not?* So she sat on the front row of the bleachers near first base.

George Walters, Will Rogers' All-State catcher, was crouched behind the plate, and about a dozen young players were gathered around the pitcher's mound. Coach McCombs stood beyond the third base foul line holding a clipboard and observing the proceedings. Since it was an informal workout before official practices began for the season, the coach wasn't supposed to get involved in the practice, but he certainly seemed intent on evaluating all the talent, or lack thereof, that might be available to him.

At one point, George stood up out of his catcher's crouch and noticed Sky sitting alone. He pulled up his mask and called, "Hey, Sky."

She mustered a smile and waved. She didn't know him very well. They shared a history class and passed in the halls occasionally, but that was about it.

He said, "Wow, I was sorry to hear about what happened to the softball team."

Sky just nodded, and he continued, "Coach wanted us to work out here on the softball field before the real tryouts next week so we don't mess up the baseball diamond."

An awkward silence stretched out between them, so George just shrugged, lowered his catcher's mask, and crouched behind the plate signaling for the next pitch.

Each of the players took their turn firing the baseball toward home plate. Most of them didn't seem to have any talent or even a clue what they were trying to do. They laughed heartily and hurled good-natured jeers and insults toward one another. A couple of the guys seemed to have pretty good arms, and Coach McCombs wrote feverishly on his clipboard as they threw their pitches.

Sky enjoyed sitting in the warm sunshine and watching the want-to-be pitchers showing their stuff. She couldn't help but lament the fact that there she was on the very field where she should have been practicing with the softball team getting ready for her senior year as the star pitcher for the Will Rogers Ropers.

As the sun began to sink in the western sky, the last aspiring young ballplayer took his place on the mound, went through an elaborate windup, and threw the ball. It bounced at least four feet in front of the plate, and George Walters displayed his catching prowess as he deftly picked it out of the dirt. Some of the other players, convinced there was nothing more to see, drifted away and headed toward the locker room.

George threw the ball back to the mound and called encouragingly, "Try it again."

Sky admired George's kind encouragement but didn't have much confidence in the young man standing atop the mound.

As he went through his comical windup motion for his second pitch, even Coach McCombs turned to go, calling, "George, whenever you guys are done here, hit the showers."

The young man hurled the baseball with all his might, but once again, it bounced in front of the plate, ricocheted off George Walter's shin guard, and bounded toward where Sky was sitting. Without even thinking about it, Sky stood up, caught the ball, and fired it back to George behind the plate. As the ball left her hand, Sky realized that all her frustration, disappointment, and anger was propelling the baseball.

It hit George Walters' catcher's mitt with a resounding *thwack* that caused Coach McCombs to whirl around and look back toward the field. He had just heard a sound that baseball coaches pray to hear but only experience a few times throughout their careers. The coach stared at the bewildered young man on the pitcher's mound then looked at his star catcher and yelled, "George, make sure that kid is on the list for the pitching tryouts."

George Walters enjoyed playing catcher more than almost anything in the world. His father had been a catcher in the Minor Leagues, so George had caught baseballs for as long as he could remember. He had been on the All-Star team the previous year and caught pitches thrown by some of the best players in the state. He had even caught baseballs thrown by some of his dad's friends who pitched in the Minor Leagues, but he was certain that the baseball he had just caught, thrown by Sky Forest, was as good as anything he had ever caught before.

Sky turned to leave as George called, "Hey, Sky. Wait up."

They walked side by side around the bleachers and toward the main school building.

George asked, "Can you meet me at the softball field tomorrow around noon? There shouldn't be anybody there on a Saturday."

Sky was confused but shrugged and asked, "What for?"

George smiled and said mysteriously, "I need you to help me check something out."

The growing darkness surrounded Sky as she walked through the neighborhood toward home. As she passed a huge old oak tree, she could have sworn she heard that peculiar voice again from behind the tree trunk, saysing, "The best is yet to come."

Chapter Three

OUT ON A LIMB

"...everybody is ignorant, only on different subjects."
—WILL ROGERS

3

Matilda paced back and forth nervously and repeatedly stared out the front window looking for Sky. It was almost dark, and her granddaughter hadn't come home yet. Matilda had tried calling her several times but couldn't get her. She thought Sky must have had her phone turned off.

Matilda absentmindedly picked up a Cherokee turkey prayer feather from a shelf near the front window. Her ancestors had used it to fan smoke during purification or healing ceremonies. Her only prayer was to have her granddaughter safely home.

Usually, Sky was mature and responsible beyond her years. Matilda trusted her in almost any situation, but today had been the day that Sky had to turn in her beloved softball uniform, and school had been out for hours.

Finally, Matilda spotted her granddaughter's graceful and athletic stride moving quickly toward home. Matilda let out a huge sigh of relief, set the prayer feather back on the shelf, and hurriedly sat in her comfortable chair near the fireplace.

As Sky burst through the front door calling, "Gram, I'm home," Matilda lowered her newspaper as if she had nothing more on her mind than a bit of casual reading.

Sky absentmindedly asked, "What's for dinner?"

Matilda was dying to find out what happened to her granddaughter at school that day and what she had been doing since classes let out, but she knew it would all come out in good time, so she just responded, "We've got some stew warming on the stove."

As they ate their dinner, Sky lamented, "Gram, everything was going to be perfect. I could have finished my senior year as an All-State softball player, and we might have even won the state championship. But now it's all gone, and I don't have anything else to do."

Matilda recited from memory, "There's a famous Cherokee proverb. 'Have patience. All things change in time. Wishing cannot bring autumn glory or cause winter to cease.'"

Sky's frustration spilled over, and she blurted, "This isn't about autumn or winter. This is about my real life."

Matilda explained, "Granddaughter, real life is a matter of making the best of what comes your way. Sometimes that which looks like chaos or crisis, in retrospect, takes on a sort of divine order."

The old woman pointed to a map that was hanging on the wall. It showed the southern part of the United States with some locations and routes marked.

She spoke, "For generations, our people lived side by side with white settlers. We experienced peace and prosperity. The future seemed to be bright. We had a written language, our own newspaper, and a constitution; but then, gold was discovered on our land, and we had to leave all our hopes and dreams behind and endure a tragic journey to a distant place where we were forced to start over again."

Sky was obviously moved by her grandmother's words but argued, "But, Gram, I don't even know what to start over doing. They took away the one thing I was good at, and now there's nothing left."

Matilda smiled patiently and explained, "Granddaughter, there's always another path, and it's impossible to know where it may take us in this life. Will Rogers, himself, dropped out of school to become a ranch hand and then discovered he was gifted at using his rope. Who could have guessed that Will's rope tricks would take him around the world and make him a popular performer, movie star, writer, and the friend of kings and presidents."

Sky nodded solemnly and offered, "Well, I am going to meet a new friend at the softball field tomorrow."

Matilda smiled knowingly, saying, "One never knows..."

The next morning, Sky was excited about meeting George at the softball field. She had no idea what he had in mind, but she gave her hair a bit of extra attention and picked out a great shirt and her best jeans.

As she approached the softball field a few minutes before noon, she noticed that George was already there waiting for her. He was sprawled out on the bench behind third base.

As Sky walked toward him, she was struck by the fact that George Walters was a big guy. She knew that in addition to being an All-State catcher who everyone thought could play in college or even the pros, he was a great linebacker on the football team who led the league in tackles.

Sky sat down a few feet away from him on the bench. George gave her the thumbs-up sign and greeted her. "Hey."

Sky responded in kind. "Hey."

There was an awkward moment between them, broken by George asking, "Is it weird for you to meet me here at the softball field after the whole thing about them getting rid of the team?"

Sky shrugged, then sighed thoughtfully and said, "It's hard to explain because I had a lot riding on this season."

George agreed. "Yeah, I know what you mean. I can't imagine what I would do if they dumped the baseball team."

Finally, the curiosity got the best of her, and Sky asked, "So... what's up?"

George reached under the bench and tossed Sky a baseball glove, saying, "Try this on."

Sky slipped the glove onto her left hand, opened and closed it a few times, then pounded her fist into the pocket.

She glanced up at George, saying, "It's a little big, but it will do."

George started putting on his catcher's equipment including his chest protector, shin guards, and his mask. He pointed toward the pitcher's mound, announcing, "I left a bagful of baseballs out there for you."

Sky was bewildered and asked, "George, couldn't you find one of the guys on the team to work out with today?"

George chuckled and responded, "No one else would work for what I have in mind."

Sky resignedly strolled out to the pitcher's mound as George took his place behind home plate.

He called out, "Just throw a couple of easy ones in here, and we'll see where we go from there."

Sky picked up a baseball and felt it settle into her hand. Although she'd been playing softball throughout her high school years, she'd grown up playing Little League baseball. She wound up with an easy motion and tossed the ball toward George's outstretched glove on the outside half of the plate. The ball plopped into the catcher's mitt exactly where George had set up for the pitch to go. George moved slightly and held his glove over the inside edge of the plate. Sky wound up and hit it again. He held his glove high and outside, and one more time, Sky's aim was true.

George tossed the ball back to her and said, "Now, let's give it a little heat."

Sky wound up and put her strength behind the pitch. Although it was faster and right over the plate, it didn't have the blazing speed her throw had exhibited the previous afternoon.

George encouraged her. "Really wind up, and let it go. Let's see your fastball."

It was a good pitch, but far from what George was hoping for.

He felt an instant inspiration, and although it required him to step out on some thin ice, he said, "Sky, don't worry about it. I didn't really think a girl could throw a fastball anyway."

Almost before George was ready, a fastball sizzled right over the middle of the plate and hit his mitt with that resounding thwack he had felt the day before.

George jumped up, pumped his fist triumphantly, and yelled, "Now that's what I'm talking about right there!"

Sky's instant flare of anger at his insult quickly faded as she understood his strategy. She found that she was able to summon the high-energy fastball at will.

George showed her how to place her fingers at different places on and around the stitches on the baseball to make her pitches curve and drop.

She asked, "How do you know all this? Did you used to pitch?"

George shook his head and explained, "No, but catchers know more about pitching and everything else that happens on the field than anyone. A lot of coaches and managers are former catchers."

Sky said, "I didn't know that."

George quipped, "There's probably a lot about catchers you don't know."

They both laughed, and the feeling was comfortable between them.

Sky said, "Let me try that inside curve again for a while."

After she had thrown three more pitches, George stood and walked toward her, announcing, "That's enough for today. You've got to save your arm."

Sky shot back, "What in the world do I need to save my arm for?"

George paused a moment to collect his thoughts, then responded, "The tryouts for pitchers is Monday afternoon at four o'clock. You'll need to meet me behind the baseball diamond at 3:45. We're going to have to approach this just right."

Sky challenged, "George, is this some sort of practical joke or bet you've got going with one of the guys?"

George seemed hurt. He sighed and explained, "Sky, this is my last chance to win a state championship, and I didn't feel very hopeful until yesterday when you caught the ball and threw it back to me like a major leaguer pitching in the World Series. The only motive I have is to get the best pitcher in our school on the baseball team."

Sky stared into George's startlingly blue eyes and saw nothing but honesty, loyalty, and maybe a little more.

Chapter Four

TRIAL BY FIRE

"A man only learns by two things.
One is reading and the other is
association with smarter people."
—WILL ROGERS

4

Sunday afternoon, Matilda and Sky were walking in the park near their home. It was one of their favorite spots in Tulsa, and spring was beginning to assert itself even though the intermittent wind still had a bit of bite.

Matilda saw a bench sitting in the sunshine and announced, "Your grandmother is going to rest her legs for a bit."

Sky sat down next to her, and they enjoyed a comfortable silence until Sky asked, "Gram, what do you think of girls doing things that are usually guy things?"

Matilda chuckled and said, "You're the second person who's ever asked me a question like that."

Sky asked, "Well, who was the first?"

Matilda responded, "Granddaughter, I am proud to say that Wilma Mankiller was a friend of mine; and as you well know, she was the principal chief of the Cherokees. There's probably nothing that is considered more of a guy thing than that."

Sky asked, "So how did she get a name like Mankiller?"

Matilda chuckled and remembered, "She got asked that question so many times I can almost remember her quote." Matilda recited, "'My name is Mankiller, and in the old Cherokee Nation, when we lived here in the Southeast, we lived in semi-autonomous villages, and there was someone who watched over the village who had the title of mankiller. And I'm not sure what you could equate that to, but it was like a soldier or someone who was responsible for the security of the village. So anyway this one fellow liked the title mankiller so well that he kept it as his name, and that's who we trace our ancestry back to.'"

Sky challenged. "So you really knew her?"

Matilda replied, "Yes, indeed. We were almost the same age, and when we were young, there were a lot more pursuits people considered guy things, and people felt a lot stronger about it than they do now."

Sky looked at her grandmother and asked, "So, what do you think?"

Matilda paused for a moment, then explained, "I never thought there were guy things or girl things. There are just things that are big challenges and people who are big enough to face them."

Sky nervously stammered, "Well, what do you think of me playing baseball on the guy's team?"

Matilda was a bit surprised, but she was able to not let it show as she answered, "What's important is not what *I* think but what *you* think.

Sky admitted, "I'm not even sure I'm good enough to play on the team, but I can't imagine how the coach, the players, and everyone else is going to take it when a girl tries out to be a pitcher on the baseball team."

Matilda smiled and said, "Since you've got me thinking about my friend Wilma becoming chief of the Cherokees, I remember her saying, 'Prior to my election, young Cherokee girls would never have thought that they might grow up and become chief.' Maybe down the road, little girls will be willing to try because Sky Forest was a great pitcher."

Sky announced, "Well, the tryout for pitchers is tomorrow at four o'clock, and I'm going to go for it."

Matilda clapped her hands and said, "Granddaughter, if I can offer one more piece of wisdom from Chief Wilma Mankiller, I remember her saying, 'I learned a long time ago that I can't control the challenges the Creator sends my way, but I can control the way I think about them and deal with them.' You didn't have anything to do with them canceling the softball team, but you can have everything to do with getting yourself on the baseball team."

Grandmother and granddaughter rose as one and walked in a companionable silence back toward their home.

As she awoke the next morning, Sky was struck by the fact that her plans that had seemed filled with possibility on a sunny Sunday afternoon in the park seemed bleak and hopeless on a dreary and blustery Monday morning.

Sky trudged to school in a daze and actually hoped that the dark clouds would produce showers in the afternoon and rain out the baseball tryouts for pitchers.

She couldn't remember one thing about her classes that day except seeing George in history class and passing him in the hall several times. He was all smiles and gave his thumbs-up gesture every time she saw him.

After her last class, Sky slipped into the girls' locker room and changed clothes for her pending tryout ordeal. She emerged from the locker room just a few minutes before she was scheduled to meet George behind the baseball stadium. Sky was wearing sweatpants, a bulky warmup jacket, a large baseball cap that hid her long black hair, and oversized sunglasses. She somehow hoped that no one would recognize her, and she wouldn't be forced to reveal her identity until the last possible moment.

As she passed the Will Rogers' statue, a voice said, "Great day for baseball."

As usual, George was early waiting for her in a clump of trees behind the left field wall of the Will Rogers Ropers baseball stadium.

He greeted her warmly. "Hey, Sky. You're going to be awesome. This will be absolutely amazing."

Sky muttered, "George, I can't believe you talked me into this."

He shot back, "Have a little faith, and follow me."

George led Sky through a gate in the outfield that was used when they brought mowers and other equipment into the stadium. They walked along the foul line into the visitors' dugout.

George pointed out a spot on the bench in the corner, explaining, "If you'll sit there in the shadows until it's your turn to pitch, no one will be able to see you over here."

George rushed across the field to the home team's dugout and got out his catcher's equipment. He was putting it on as Coach McCombs and a number of players began wandering onto the field.

The only people required to be at the tryout were new pitchers trying to make the team and George who would be catching for them; but as four o'clock approached, most of the baseball team was there to observe from the field, and a number of students and fans seemed to be gathering in the stands. George noticed that the three wealthy Tulsa businessmen who supported the team and came to every game were in their seats below the press box. Everyone called them The Trio because they were always together and had sponsored the team generously for years.

The coach had posted a sheet on the wall of the dugout listing the names of the five players who had signed up to try out. George had scribbled the name *Forest* under the fifth name.

Coach McCombs stepped into the dugout, slapped George on the back warmly, and inquired, "Well, George, are we about ready to get this thing started?"

George responded enthusiastically, "Yes, sir."

As the coach glanced at the list on the wall, George rushed to take his place behind home plate.

He greeted several of his teammates. Ken and Patrick Couples, who played left field and right field, as usual were together standing behind first base. They were identical twins, and no one could ever tell them apart, so George just waved and said, "Hey, guys."

Bob Dewitt, the Ropers' third baseman and team prankster, was standing behind the plate and acting like he was going to be the umpire for the tryout.

Sky's nervous feelings were building toward terror as the coach called for the first would-be pitcher.

Tim Eddings was a small redheaded kid who had tried out the previous year and could hardly get the ball to the plate. The coach nodded and tried to be encouraging, saying, "Well, let's see what you've got for us this year."

Eddings wound up to pitch but was so off balance he had to catch himself before he fell down, and had to start his windup over.

Bob Dewitt, who was still presiding as a mock umpire behind the plate, quipped, "What's that? A new dance step?"

The coach shot him a dirty look, but it was obvious everyone was trying to stifle laughter.

After a couple of weak pitches landed somewhere around the plate, Coach McCombs patted Tim Eddings on the back and said, "Thanks for coming by. I can sure tell you've been working on it."

The second pitcher to try out was a freshman named Dave Wildasin. He had a strong arm but needed to work on his control as his pitches had tremendous velocity but often missed the plate by several feet.

When a ball whistled by Bob Dewitt's head, he decided it would be a good time to give up his mock umpire act.

George overheard the coach say to one of his assistants, "The Wildasin kid could be a real player for us in a year or two but probably won't contribute this year."

The third and fourth aspiring pitchers to try out obviously had the desire to play but lacked the talent. They were politely and promptly dismissed.

The fifth pitcher to try out took his place on the mound. His name was Bill Shelton. He was an outstanding middleweight wrestler on Will Rogers High's wrestling team and threw the baseball with good control as all his pitches were over the plate, but he had no speed or power.

Coach McCombs said to one of his assistants, "He might work out to throw batting practice, but I'm afraid he would get us killed in a game."

The assistant coach responded, "Yeah, but we've got to have another pitcher, and he may be our best alternative."

Coach McCombs slapped his clipboard against his leg and lamented, "We've got a great team, and I believe we're just one good pitcher away from a state championship. I was hoping for..."

The coach looked down at his list noticing the name *Forest* written below the five names that had been printed. He turned to his assistant and asked, "Who's Forest?"

The assistant coach shrugged and replied, "I haven't got a clue."

Coach McCombs looked around the field and called, "Anybody know a kid named Forest? I don't have a last name."

Bob Dewitt called, "Maybe it's Forest Gump. That's who we need on the mound."

Everyone laughed.

The coach shrugged, saying, "I guess that's it then."

Everybody started to leave, but paused as George called to the coach, "Hey, coach. Remember the pitcher who threw that fastball when we were working out over on the softball field and you wanted me to get the name on the list?"

The coach nodded enthusiastically. "Yeah, I remember, George. Where's that kid?"

George signaled toward the visitors' dugout, and Sky emerged, trudging toward the pitcher's mound. Everyone on the field and in the stands fell silent. Even with the warmup jacket, hat, and glasses, it was obvious to everyone that something wasn't right.

Coach McCombs swung around toward George and bellowed, "Walters, what's going on here, and who's this?"

George paused, took a deep breath, and explained, "Coach, this is Forest, Sky Forest, who threw that fastball over on the softball field."

The coach shook his head indignantly and yelled, "George, this isn't funny. That's it for tryouts. I'll see everyone at practice tomorrow."

In a voice that could be heard throughout the stadium and quite a bit farther, George Walters yelled, "Stop!"

Chapter Five

A Moment of Truth

"Heroes are made every little while, but only one in a million conduct themselves afterwards so that it makes us proud that we honored them at the time."
—WILL ROGERS

5

Everyone on the field fell silent, and nobody moved. All the people in the stands remained motionless, and not a word was uttered. For all Sky Forest knew as she stood on the pitcher's mound, the whole world had just screeched to a silent halt.

George Walters defiantly strode to Coach McCombs and emphatically stated, "Coach, for three years, I've given you my blood, sweat, and tears. There's no one who has worked harder for you than I have. I've done everything you've asked me to and more."

The coach solemnly nodded and agreed, "You're right, son."

George concluded, "If I can give you three years, I don't think it's too much to ask for you to give me three minutes."

The coach glanced from George to Sky and back, then announced, "Let's do this." He shrugged and muttered, "I don't know what the rule book says, but it's probably not going to matter anyway."

George trotted back to the plate and crouched behind it. He pounded his mitt and called, "Okay, Sky, fire it right in here."

Sky was terrified but somehow went through a semblance of a windup and awkwardly threw the ball. It slipped out of her hand and sailed five feet over George's head and hit the backstop. Everyone in the stadium broke into uproarious laughter. Sky turned her back on them, determined not to let them see her cry.

Then it happened. He was standing there right in front of her. It was Will Rogers, himself, smiling at her and wearing his rumpled suit and his battered hat tipped back on his head.

He chuckled and said, "Well, this is quite a situation we've got here." He seemed to shimmer and glow as he continued, "It was always my experience that you start out with folks laughin' *at* you, but with a little work, they start laughin' *with* you, and with a lot more work and a bit of luck, they start laughin' at themselves."

Sky was speechless, and finally managed to shrug. She glanced around the field and up into the stands realizing that no one was seeing what she was seeing.

Will observed, "I found my path in life through a rope, and right now, I suspect you're gonna find your path through a baseball." Will scratched his head, gave her a lopsided grin and concluded. "If I were you, I'd give 'em the fastball. Just wind up nice and easy and watch your release point."

Sky felt George's hand on her shoulder. He said, "Sky, let's try it again. Just relax during your windup, watch your release point, and throw the fastball."

Sky glanced back toward where Will Rogers had been standing, but there was nothing between her and the flagpole in center field but a lot of bright green grass.

As she turned to stare toward home plate, the laughter turned into taunts and jeers. "The squaw wants to play ball with the braves." "She throws like a girl!" And, "Run home to your teepee."

Sky tried to block it all out of her mind and channeled her anger and frustration into the pitch. A calm fell over her as she wound up and let the ball fly. The resounding thwack that echoed throughout the stadium silenced everyone.

Then whispers could be heard. "Did you see that?" "What in the world?" And, "I've never seen anything like it."

George was ecstatic but tried to act as if he had expected it all along. He tossed the ball back to Sky and called, "Okay, Sky. Let's do it again."

George held his mitt waist high over the outside edge of the plate, and Sky threw it like an arrow hitting the target.

George yelled, "Let's see anybody try to hit that."

He tossed the ball back to Sky and prompted, "Okay. Now let's let the curve ball loose."

Sky adjusted her fingers across the stitches on the baseball and snapped her wrist as she let go of the ball. It looked like it was going to be more than a foot outside, but at the last instant, it turned and dove right over the plate.

Coach McCombs stepped onto the mound and confirmed, "So your name is Sky Forest, and you go to school here?"

Sky just nodded.

He motioned for George to join them on the mound and said, "Well, young lady, I don't know how we're going to do it or what's going to happen, but welcome to the Rogers Ropers baseball team."

The coach extended his hand to Sky, and she timidly shook it.

George spoke up. "Thanks, coach."

The coach shook his head and said, "No, son. Thank you. Obviously, this old coach still has a few things to learn."

The coach turned back toward Sky, saying, "Practice starts tomorrow. Three o'clock sharp on this field." Then the coach turned and walked away.

George hugged Sky, picked her up off the ground, and spun her around a complete circle. He put her back down and said, "You did it! That was absolutely awesome."

Only then did Sky notice the other players on the team gathering around them as everyone in the stands stood and cheered.

The Couples twins shook Sky's hand, one of them saying, "We're Ken and Patrick."

The other twin added, "We'll both answer to either name. Welcome to the team."

David Allen, the six-foot-six center fielder towered over Sky and said, "I'm glad you're on *our* team. I'd hate to try to hit that curve ball."

Bob Dewitt patted Sky on the back and said, "Well, now that you're on the team, I'll make sure you get a locker next to mine… It will certainly liven up things in the shower."

George playfully kicked Bob on the backside and quipped, "Get out of here."

The shortstop, Fernando Cruz, greeted Sky, "Wow. It's great to have you with us."

Michael Fenner, the team's second baseman, seemed shy, awkward, and nervous. He nodded, pointed toward Fernando, and just blurted, "Yeah, what he said."

Cletus Jefferson, the team's first baseman, was an All-State power forward on the Will Rogers basketball team. A broad grin broke out across his ebony face, and he said, "Anybody gives you any hassle or lip, just let me know."

Sky never wanted the moment to end. She stood there with George as the stadium emptied.

Finally, they turned to walk toward the dugout and noticed several people gathered on the front row of the stands. Sky looked closer and saw that it was The Trio standing there in their business suits next to her grandmother who was smiling at Sky with a few tears rolling down her face.

As Sky and George reached the edge of the bleachers, one of the businessmen extended his hand to Sky and shook her hand enthusiastically. He proclaimed, "We want to thank you for giving us an unforgettable afternoon, and we were wondering if you could join us for dinner."

Sky turned toward her grandmother who simply nodded *Yes*. Then she glanced at George and asked the businessman, "Grandma and George, too?

The businessman laughed heartily and assured her, "Absolutely."

Since George and Sky needed to change, everyone agreed to meet at the front entrance of the school in fifteen minutes.

George headed toward the boys' locker room as Sky and her grandmother strolled toward the other end of the building.

Sky observed, "You didn't tell me you were going to be here."

Matilda chuckled and stated, "Granddaughter, I've lived through almost eighty baseball seasons, and believe it or not, I've never been to a tryout for pitchers, so I thought I'd better take this opportunity."

Sky sighed and responded, "It's probably just as well I didn't know you were there because I was already scared to death."

Sky stopped walking, and her grandmother turned toward her curiously. Sky looked off into the distance and asked, "Gram, do you believe Will Rogers could actually appear in front of you and talk to you?"

Matilda could tell that her granddaughter was serious, so she stated solemnly, "Sky, I believe our ancestors have gone before us to show us the path and help us along the way. Will Rogers was the most famous Cherokee of his time and arguably the most famous Cherokee of any time. I think his words and his example had a lot to say then, just like they do now."

Sky nodded emotionally and responded, "Thanks, Gram."

As they continued walking, Sky asked, "What do you think the businessmen want?"

Matilda answered, "Most of us eat because we're hungry for food. Sometimes businesspeople eat because they're hungry for business."

Sky was bewildered and blurted, "Gram, I don't have any business to offer them."

Matilda chuckled wisely and said, "Granddaughter, you might be surprised."

Chapter Six

RESTORATION AND RENEWAL

*"America is a land of opportunity
and don't ever forget it."*
—WILL ROGERS

6

Sky hurried into the girls' locker room to get changed so she could meet everyone for dinner. As she sat on the bench in front of her locker, it was hard for her to believe that she had sat in this same spot a little over an hour before, but now, the whole world had changed.

She took an extra few moments to touch up her makeup and check everything out in the mirror. It wasn't every day a girl got to dine with three of the city's most prominent businessmen, her grandmother, and last but not least, George.

As she hurried down the hallway toward the front of the school, she came in sight of the Will Rogers' statue and veered toward it. She paused in front of old Will and looked up at him. After a moment, she whispered, "Thanks for showing up when you did." She waited a moment and giggled, "Oh, so now you've got nothing to say for yourself?"

Sky turned and hurried to the front door. Just as she reached it, she heard, "The best is yet to come."

Sky didn't even turn around knowing that no one would be behind her other than Will Rogers.

Matilda and George were waiting for Sky on the sidewalk, and behind them was a gleaming white stretch limousine with a chauffeur holding the back door open for them.

George remarked, "I was just hoping to catch a ride home with one of the guys."

Matilda added, "Well, I was just going to walk home."

She turned and greeted the chauffeur. "My name is Matilda Forest."

He took her hand solemnly, saying, "Yes, ma'am. I'm Michael, and I'll be honored to drive you this evening.

Matilda slid into the back seat of the limousine.

George timidly reached into his pocket for his cell phone. He shyly asked the chauffeur, "Michael, would you mind taking our picture? It might be a long time before we get to ride in another limousine like this."

Michael nodded respectfully and reached for the cell phone as if it were something he did every day. George slipped his arm around Sky, and they posed standing next to the limousine.

Michael said, "I don't know. The way you two play baseball, you may have to get used to riding around in limousines."

Sky and George smiled, and Michael took their picture.

When Sky and George settled into the back seat next to Matilda, they noticed the three businessmen sitting in a seat facing toward them.

One of them asked, "Do you folks like Italian food?"

Matilda nodded and said, "Fine."

Sky added, "Sounds good."

George chimed in, "I'll eat anything that doesn't eat me first."

Everyone laughed, and the businessman turned toward the front of the limousine and said, "Michael, take us to Ti Amo's, please."

When he turned back around, he said, "I just realized we haven't been formally introduced. My name is Wayne Johnstone, and I'm an investment banker. Sitting in the middle here is William Koslow. He runs a construction company, and we all call him Billy. Then on the far side is Everett Tally. He's in the oil business.

He started out with just one well, and now I think he owns almost all of them."

Everyone laughed comfortably, and Everett Tally got back at Wayne Johnstone, saying, "Wayne over there claims to be an investment banker, but the way it works is he loans money to people who don't need it and opens savings accounts for everyone else."

The good-natured laughter continued.

Mr. Koslow spoke to George. "Son, the three of us played baseball for Will Rogers High School about a hundred years ago."

As everyone chuckled, he continued. "We really enjoyed watching you the last couple of years, and I'm curious whether you're planning to play in college or maybe go pro."

George paused a moment and responded, "Thank you, sir. The only plans I have are to do the best I can this year and see what comes after that."

Mr. Johnstone stated, "A wise approach, I believe."

The other businessmen nodded their agreement.

Wayne Johnstone focused on Sky and asked, "Young lady, what are *your* plans?"

Sky shrugged and admitted, "I don't have a clue. A few days ago, I was planning to start my senior year playing on the softball team, and now my whole world is turned upside down."

The businessman nodded and responded, "Yes, I can see that. It's sort of why we wanted to get together with you all this evening."

Michael piloted the stretch limousine through downtown Tulsa, and the car seemed to float above the roadway. It only took a few minutes, and Michael stopped the car in front of the restaurant, jumped out, and rushed to open the back door.

The owner of the restaurant stepped outside to hold open the front door and introduced himself to Matilda, Sky, and George. "My name is Mehdi. Welcome to Ti Amo's."

He turned to the businessmen and announced, "Gentlemen, the boardroom is ready just as you requested."

In a few moments, everyone was settled around a long table in a comfortable private room.

An efficient and somewhat formal waiter rushed into the room, handed everyone menus, and informed them of the daily specials. After everyone had placed their orders, the waiter quietly exited, closing the door to the boardroom behind him.

The three businessmen glanced at one another and seemed to come to some type of consensus.

Wayne Johnstone began. "As Billy mentioned in the car, the three of us played baseball at Will Rogers High School and have remained friends ever since." He paused for a moment, smiled, and quipped, "Well if we're going to be totally candid here, Everett and I played baseball, and Billy sat on the bench."

Everyone laughed.

Everett Tally added, "That's not fair. He didn't just sit on the bench. He carried all the equipment."

When the laughter died down, Wayne Johnstone continued. "We never miss a game and rarely miss a practice; but today, we saw something we've never seen before, and it's going to create a lot of challenges and opportunities this season."

He focused directly on Sky and resumed. "Sky, there's going to be a lot of publicity and media hype about you playing baseball with the guys. Some of the school board officials and fans of the opposing teams may not be fully on board in the beginning. It could get a little difficult, and we want to do whatever we can to smooth the way for you."

Sky stammered, "I don't have any idea what I might want or need."

Mr. Johnstone glanced toward Matilda and asked, "Mrs. Forest, what are your thoughts?"

Matilda respected the three businessmen but was in no way intimidated. She stated, "My granddaughter is a formidable young lady who has dealt with adversity throughout her life. She lost her parents as an infant, and I am a rather traditional Cherokee Indian, so she has had to grow up with one foot in two different worlds. It's hard enough to be a teenager under normal conditions, but she has somehow gathered the best of both worlds and brought it all into her life.

"We appreciate your support, encouragement, and generosity, but I think you will find Sky to be both resilient and autonomous; but rest assured, we will reach out to you as needed."

Everett Tally nodded and addressed Matilda, saying, "Ma'am, have you ever thought about being on the board of an oil company?"

Everyone laughed, but Mr. Tally responded, "I'm not kidding."

As their meals were served, they all spoke pleasantly about baseball and Will Rogers High School.

Billy Koslow told everyone that Will Rogers, himself, had been a huge baseball fan and actually attended the World Series in 1934 when Detroit played St. Louis. He explained, "Will was in town performing where he had previously appeared at the St. Louis World's Fair. He went over to catch the Cardinals playing the Tigers in the series. From then on, he was hooked and would catch a game wherever his travels took him. He and his vaudeville troop formed their own baseball team and would play other performers every time they got the chance."

As the dinner drew to a close, Mr. Johnstone reminded Sky, "Just let us know if you need anything."

Sky hesitated for a moment, then stated, "If you're really serious, there is one thing you could do for me."

The room fell silent as everyone stared at Sky. She said, "I would like to see the softball team restored."

The three longtime friends and businessmen glanced toward one another, nodded, and smiled.

Everett Tally announced, "We'll have to work out the details, but it seems like some type of sponsorship for the softball team this year would be in order."

He looked toward Sky and continued, "This would, of course, be assuming that you're going to remain as the ace pitcher on the Roper's baseball team."

Sky nodded, smiled broadly, and responded, "Gentlemen, I believe we have a deal."

Chapter Seven

PAST, PRESENT, AND FUTURE

"We will never have true civilization until we have learned to recognize the rights of others."
—WILL ROGERS

7

Michael stopped the limousine in front of Matilda and Sky's home. He held the door open for them.

Matilda looked at the three businessmen and said, "Gentlemen, you have made a really amazing day even more special for us."

She said goodnight to George and slid out of the car.

Sky hugged George and whispered, "Thanks for everything. See you tomorrow."

She stepped out of the limousine where Michael said, "Good night," to both Sky and Matilda. They walked toward their house.

Sky felt as if she were walking on clouds. She exclaimed, "Gram, there are so many unbelievable things happening, I don't even know what to think about."

Matilda patted her granddaughter on the shoulder and said, "Yes, I understand, but there's always one thing you should think about that will help to guide all your decisions now and in the future."

Sky stopped on the front porch and turned toward her grandmother.

Matilda explained, "Granddaughter, all of us are on paths throughout our lives. We must always seek to follow the right path. Never walk on a path that doesn't go where you want to be or follow anyone who is not the kind of person you want to become."

Sky nodded and replied, "Yes, I understand."

Matilda continued, "You are one of the special people who breaks new ground and creates the path. You must always be mindful of the fact that you're not merely traveling for yourself, but you're creating a path for others to follow."

Sky asked, "Do you mean baseball?"

Matilda nodded and answered, "Yes, I mean baseball and everything else in your life. Sometime in the future, there will be other girls who may want to play baseball or do other things the world may not be ready to accept just yet. The fact that they will be following in your path will make all the difference. None of us succeed on our own. We benefit or suffer the consequences of the actions of those who have gone before us."

Sky was bewildered and argued, "But there's never been a girl play baseball at Will Rogers High School."

Matilda nodded and concluded, "Yes, I understand, but there was a time when girls—particularly Cherokee girls—didn't get to go to school at all. Then someone was the first to do it, and now you are following their path."

Sky hugged their grandmother, and they both went into the house.

If Sky wasn't already certain that her world had changed, the scene that greeted her as she walked toward school the next morning would have convinced her. There were reporters, news vans, and a crowd of people milling around in front of the main door to the school. The excitement built, and the sound grew as the mob noticed Sky Forest walking toward them. People reached out toward her, and reporters started shouting questions.

Sky was about to panic when she noticed David Allen walking beside her on her left and Cletus Jefferson on her right.

David looked down at Sky and greeted her. "Good morning, Sky. We thought you might enjoy a little company walking to school this morning."

Cletus cleared a path in front of them shouting, "Back up. No comment."

They made it safely through the front door, and Sky turned to David and Cletus, saying, "Thanks, guys. I don't know what I would have done without you."

Cletus responded, "Don't thank us. You're part of the team, and we're family."

Sky waved at them as they each headed toward their first class of the day.

Sky glanced up at the statue of Will Rogers and murmured, "Good morning."

She turned to rush to her first class fearing she might be late.

A voice behind her said, "Good morning to you. It looks like the insanity is starting kind of the way it happened to me. Don't be late for history class. It's really going to be great today."

Sky slipped into her class just as her history teacher, Mrs. Harris, was closing the door.

Sky blurted, "Good morning. Sorry I'm late. Someone was talking to me in the hall."

Mrs. Harris was one of Sky's favorite teachers and made history both fun and interesting. She responded, "Don't worry about it. Take your seat, and we'll get started."

Mrs. Harris walked to the front of the classroom, greeted everyone, and began. "Today, we're going to continue our discussion of the most influential figures at the beginning of the twentieth century."

Students shuffled books and papers as they settled in for the lecture.

Mrs. Harris continued, "Today, we're going to focus on arguably the most famous man of his time who influenced every area of life in the United States and around the world."

She glanced around her classroom and asked, "Anybody care to venture a guess?"

Sky timidly raised her hand, and Mrs. Harris nodded at her.

Sky spoke hopefully. "Will Rogers?"

Mrs. Harris smiled and stated, "You're absolutely right. I know we all take it for granted around here because we use Will Rogers' name constantly because this is our school; but Will Rogers came from humble beginnings and changed the whole world."

Mrs. Harris moved to the board in front of the room and created a timeline as she spoke. "Will was born in 1879 near here in Rogers County. Many people mistakenly think Rogers County was named for Will, but it was actually named after his father, Clem Rogers, who was a prominent rancher of the day. When Will was born, Oklahoma was not a state yet, so this was all Indian Territory. This is significant because Will was a Cherokee Indian, a fact he took great pride in all his life.

"In 1898, Will began to work on a ranch in Texas. He never enjoyed the work, but found he had tremendous talent and great skill using a rope. Will's rope would make him famous and take him around the world."

Mrs. Harris continued writing on the board and said, "In 1902, Will Rogers was in Africa as a performer in Texas Jack's American Circus and Wild West Show. He was billed as the Cherokee Kid. In 1904, Will performed his rope tricks at the World's Fair in St. Louis.

"In 1905, Will got a lot of publicity and notoriety for lassoing a bull that had escaped into the crowd during a show at Madison Square Garden in New York City. In 1908, Will married Betty Blake, and they eventually had four children.

"In 1915, Will Rogers took his first airplane ride. This would be a significant part of his life as well as his death. He was a pioneer in the aviation industry. In 1916, Will gave his first presidential performance for Woodrow Wilson, and later that year, he joined the Ziegfeld Follies as a featured performer.

"In 1918, Will made his first motion picture. He eventually starred in more than seventy films. In 1922, Will began writing a weekly newspaper column; and then in 1926, he added a daily column. These two columns combined were available to one-third of Americans and continued throughout the remainder of his life. In 1925, he began touring the country giving lectures. In 1926, he was elected the honorary mayor of Beverly Hills, California.

"In 1930, Will Rogers began a series of radio broadcasts that brought him more fame and popularity across the country. In 1931, he traveled to Nicaragua to benefit earthquake and fire victims, then he traveled to London in 1932 for a disarmament conference. In 1933, Will was recognized as the highest paid film star in Hollywood, and along with his radio broadcasts and newspaper columns, made him the most popular and beloved figure of the day."

Mrs. Harris moved away from the board, sat on the edge of her desk, and concluded, "In 1935, Will Rogers and his flying companion, Wiley Post, were tragically killed in a plane crash in Alaska. The whole world mourned his passing."

Mrs. Harris shuffled through several papers on her desk and found the one she was looking for. She explained, "When Will was asked how he wanted to be remembered, he said, 'When I die, my epitaph or whatever you call those signs on gravestones, is going to read *I joked about every prominent man of my time, but I never met a man I dident like. I am proud of that that I can hardly wait to die so it can be carved. And when you come to my grave, you will probably find me sitting there proudly reading it.'"

The bell rang signaling the end of class. All the other kids rushed out into the hall leaving Sky and Mrs. Harris behind.

Mrs. Harris glanced toward Sky and inquired, "Was there anything else, Sky?"

Sky shook her head and replied, "No, ma'am. I was just thinking about what Will Rogers did and said."

Mrs. Harris observed, "Yes, and it's almost like he's still around influencing us today."

Sky got up to leave, nodded, and replied, "You've got that right."

Chapter Eight

WORK AND PLAY

"Baseball is our national game; every boy and girl in the United States should play it. It should be made compulsory in the schools."
—WILL ROGERS

8

That first day of baseball practice was really tough for Sky. They didn't have a baseball uniform that fit her, so she had a choice between looking like a resale clothing store reject or looking like a little kid wearing their dad's uniform.

When Coach McCombs learned of Sky's dilemma, he approached the equipment managers and yelled, "I expect you guys to get Forest a uniform that fits and looks good, and I want it fast."

It took a couple of days, but the equipment managers did their magic, and Sky had the perfect baseball uniform.

She felt somewhat comfortable with her pitching, but she had focused so much on it that as practice began she panicked realizing that she was going to have to bat, too. Each of the players took their turn in the mesh cage for batting practice. Then they all just hung around waiting to watch Sky take her turn for her first time at bat.

George stayed close to Sky and called to all his teammates, "Hey, guys. Let's give Sky a break and get out on the diamond to work on your fielding or something."

The other players drifted away but kept an eye on Sky as she stepped into the batter's cage.

One of the assistant coaches threw batting practice. It was his job to throw a relatively slow pitch in the strike zone so players could work on their swing and practice making contact with the ball.

Sky missed the first few pitches by a mile. She was getting more frustrated with each toss of the ball.

George signaled to the assistant coach, stepped into the cage, and said, "Wait a minute."

He turned to Sky and spoke softly. "You're trying too hard. You don't have to kill the ball."

George demonstrated his footwork and how he shifted his weight when he swung the bat. He nodded to Sky saying, "Now, you try it."

George nodded to the assistant coach who lobbed the next pitch toward Sky. She promptly hit a line drive over his head. Then she fouled off a few pitches but seemed to get the hang of it and ended her batting practice session with several good hits in a row.

She turned to George, smiled, and said, "I don't know what I'd do without you."

George replied, "Well, let's hope you don't have to find out. Besides, pitchers and catchers have to stick together."

Coach McCombs was pleased with Sky's fielding and base running, but he knew there were still a lot of details to work out, and there was going to be an unbelievable amount of pressure on Sky when they played their season opener in less than two weeks.

After practice, Sky hurried to get showered and changed so she could attend the impromptu farewell to softball party that evening.

In spite of her best efforts to hurry, as Sky arrived, she noticed she was the last softball player to join the party.

She greeted and hugged her friends and former teammates. Kelly, Crystal, and Brandi were sitting in the corner, and they waved for her to join them. Everyone seemed glad to see Sky, and they all were in a bright and cheerful mood, especially for a group that had just lost their softball team.

The party atmosphere was shattered when Shelly looked at Sky and spoke loud enough for all to hear, "Well, there's the traitor. She finally decided to show up."

A silence fell over the room, and Sally said, "Sky's not a traitor. She worked as hard as the rest of us, and she lost her chance to play softball like everyone else did."

Shelly shot back, "Yeah, but she didn't waste any time dumping us and rushing over to the baseball team."

Shelly was one of those people who always complained and could find fault in every situation. She blurted, "Sky, I thought you Indians respected your tribe and stuck together better than this."

Several of the girls turned away from Shelly wanting to avoid her wrath, but Tamara stepped forward and put her arm around Sky's shoulder. Tamara looked like a young Diana Ross and always seemed to be able to say the right thing at the right time.

Tamara turned to Shelly and said, "Shelly, it's not right or fair for you to question what Sky does or her loyalty to her Cherokee heritage."

Shelly objected. "Tamara, why don't you just stay out of it? What do you know about the Cherokee Indians anyway?"

Tamara smiled angelically and responded, "Shelly, as usual, you put your foot in your mouth. If it's any of your business, I am a Cherokee Indian."

Shelly laughed haughtily and spat, "I didn't realize there were any Indian tribes in Africa."

Tamara explained, "Well, if you really want to know, my ancestors came here in chains in the bottom of slave ships. Then in 1864, President Lincoln signed the Emancipation Proclamation which freed the slaves, but it would be a century before the United States passed the civil rights amendment giving our people equal rights under the U.S. law; but shortly after the Emancipation Proclamation, slaves who had been owned by Cherokee Indian families were recognized by a legal term known as Freedmen and became part of the tribe. Although there have been a lot of court battles throughout the years, my family is so intermarried and intertwined with the Cherokee tribe, I consider it an important part of my heritage."

Shelly challenged, "Well, what percentage Cherokee Indian are you?"

Jenny, who was lovingly thought of as the school's student historian, offered, "Since Will Rogers, himself, was a Cherokee Indian and since I've gotten to know both Sky and Tamara, I've studied this a lot. A prominent Cherokee tribal leader may have put it best when he said, 'It isn't the quantity of Cherokee blood in your veins that is important but the quality of it...your pride in it. I have seen full-bloods who have virtually no idea of the great legacy entrusted to their care. Yet, I have seen people with as little as 1/500th blood quantum who inspire the spirits of their ancestors because they make being Cherokee a proud part of their everyday life.'

"And our own Will Rogers may have put it best when he was asked whether he was a true American citizen, saying, 'My ancestors didn't come over on the Mayflower, but they met the boat when it landed.' So, it's as much a matter of spirit, respect, and tradition as it is bloodline and ancestry."

Shelly glared at Jenny and said, "Well, I don't have time for any more of your lectures. I'm preparing for the softball protest at the school assembly on Friday."

Brandi asked, "Are you going to try to get the softball team reinstated?"

Shelly shook her head violently and declared, "No way. We are going to be marching, picketing, and protesting to get the baseball team cut from the budget. What's good for the goose is good for the gander."

Kelly chimed in. "Shelly, you've got to be kidding. What good does it do us if the guys don't get to play baseball?"

Shelly retorted, "My view is if *we* don't play, *nobody* plays, and I want you all to join in my protest."

Sky knew that the three businessmen who made up The Trio were working on restoring the softball team, and they were planning to be at the assembly on Friday, but she had promised to keep it confidential until they worked out all the details and made the formal announcement. So, Sky just turned to Shelly and suggested, "Shelly, why don't you hold off till next week and see what happens."

Shelly stamped her foot in anger and demanded, "Why in the world would I waste time just to wait and see what might happen?"

Sky answered, "Because, Shelly, you're going to make a fool out of yourself."

Crystal added, "Well, that's what usually happens to Shelly. She's probably used to it by now."

Everyone laughed as Shelly stormed out of the room.

Chapter Nine

LEADERS AND POLITICIANS

*"Everything is changing in America.
People are taking their comedians
seriously and the politicians as a joke,
when it used to be visa versa."*
—WILL ROGERS

9

The next day, Sky got a real lesson on the difference between government officials, politicians, and true leaders. It all began in her political science class as Mr. Stamps was discussing the impact of popular culture on politics and government.

He explained, "There has probably never been a private citizen that ever impacted the U.S. government policy and American politics as much as our own Will Rogers. He befriended most of the presidents and prominent politicians in the early twentieth century even though he ridiculed them in print and during his radio broadcasts. Will Rogers had the temperament and talent to critique and even make fun of leaders without getting mean-spirited. It's something we could sorely use in our world today."

Mr. Stamps stepped over to a bookshelf and withdrew a thick, leather-bound volume.

He said, "These are all quotes from Will Rogers."

He turned a few pages, then read aloud the following Will Rogers quotes:

- "I don't belong to any organized political faith. I am a Democrat."

- "Remember, write to your Congressman. Even if he can't read, write to him."

- "Why don't they pass a Constitutional Amendment prohibiting anybody learning anything? And if it works as good as the Prohibition one did, in five years we would have the smartest race of people on Earth."

- "You know it takes nerve to be a Democrat. But it takes money to be a Republican."

- "The Democrats take the whole thing as a joke and the Republicans take it serious, but run it like a joke."

- "You know the platform will always be the same, promise everything, deliver nothing."

- "I have a scheme for stopping war. It's this—no nation is allowed to enter a war till they've paid for the last one."

- "Well the elections will be breaking out pretty soon, and a flock of Democrats will replace a mess of Republicans in quite a few districts. It won't mean a thing, they will go in like all the rest of 'em, go in on promises and come out on alibis."

- "The Republicans mopped up, the Democrats gummed up, and I will now try and sum up. Things are terrible dull now. We won't have any more comedy until Congress meets."

- "I bet after seeing us, [George Washington] would sue us for calling him Father."

- "If by some divine act of providence we could get rid of both these parties and hired some good men, like any other business does, why that would be sitting pretty."

- "You know, the more you read and observe about this politics thing, you got to admit that each party is worse than the other. The one that's out always looks the best."

Mr. Stamps closed the book and set it back on the shelf, saying, "That barely begins to scratch the surface of Will's commentary on politics and politicians. Somehow, he managed to criticize the actions of our leaders without making it seem like a personal attack on them individually.

"Will Rogers actually got involved in an entire political campaign that was a parody but may have given the country the relief and a few laughs that were desperately needed at the time. It was in 1928 when President Calvin Coolidge was asked if he was going to run for re-election. He let everyone in the country know that he did not choose to run, which opened the door for Herbert Hoover to become the nominee. On the Democratic side, Al Smith got the nomination.

"A lot of political writers and pundits felt it was destined to be a boring political season, so Robert Sherwood, the editor of a weekly humor magazine, called for a third candidate. Will Rogers suggested calling it the No-Bunk campaign, and his idea was so popular he was nominated as the make-believe party's candidate.

"Will attended both the Republican and Democratic conventions, not only as a reporter but as a mock campaign opponent. He called on both Hoover and Smith to debate him but received no response. Will Rogers' memorable campaign slogan was, 'If I'm elected, I will resign.'"

Mr. Stamps looked at the students seated in front of him and asked, "How would you compare what Will Rogers did in 1928 with what's going on in our country now?"

Jenny offered, "What Will Rogers did was funny but didn't seem so personal or vindictive."

Mr. Stamps nodded encouragingly and prompted, "Anyone else?"

Sky chimed in, "Will made as much fun of himself as anyone else."

As the bell signaled the end of class, the principal of the school, Mr. Stanley, came into the classroom and whispered something to Mr. Stamps who called, "Sky, can you stay behind for a moment?"

After all her classmates were gone, Sky was left standing in front of her teacher and principal. She felt a bit nervous as she waited for an explanation.

Principal Stanley spoke. "Sky, the school board is convening a special session here in our building this afternoon, and they've requested to see Coach McCombs, your grandmother, and you. We've already called your grandmother, and she will meet us in the conference room in about twenty minutes."

Sky couldn't imagine what awaited her in the meeting, but she had a looming sense that it wasn't going to be good.

The conference room had a long table that stretched the length of the room with a podium at one end. There was a severe-looking man in a black suit standing behind the podium as Sky entered. She noticed her grandmother seated at the other end of the table and slid into a chair next to her. Matilda reached out and grasped her granddaughter's hand.

Sky asked, "Gram, did they tell you what's going on?"

Matilda shook her head and replied, "No, they just told me it concerned you, and they asked me to be here."

Principal Stanley walked into the conference room with Coach McCombs. The coach sat down next to Sky as the principal walked to the head of the table and shook hands with the man who had been standing there.

Coach McCombs patted Sky's arm and tried to offer some encouragement. "Keep your chin up, kid. The good guys always win."

A number of other men and women wearing business attire entered the conference room and found seats around the table.

Principal Stanley welcomed everyone from the podium. "Good afternoon. We are proud to have this special meeting of the school board here at Will Rogers High School. I am Principal Stanley. I'm not really sure what this is about, so at this time, I'm going to turn it over to the chairman of the school board, Herbert Schmidt."

Schmidt gripped the podium and glared down the length of the table. He cleared his throat and spoke formally. "As mentioned, I am Chairman Herbert Schmidt of the school board. Arrayed around the table are the other members of the board. We have called this emergency session to deal with a critical issue that is quite timely."

Schmidt paused for emphasis.

A well-dressed, distinguished man, entered the conference room and sat next to Matilda. As he whispered to her, Schmidt shuffled through a few notes, and continued, "It has come to our attention from concerned faculty, staff, parents, and students that this school's athletic department has broken with protocol, tradition, and the rule of order."

Coach McCombs interrupted, "Where are we heading here?"

Schmidt glared at the coach and demanded, "Who are you, sir?"

The coach responded, "I am Wayne McCombs, head baseball coach here at Will Rogers High School."

Schmidt smiled malevolently and proclaimed, "Ah, yes. You, sir, are at the center of the controversy."

Principal Stanley intervened attempting to be a peacemaker. "Chairman Schmidt, possibly you can give us some details surrounding the matter you are citing."

Schmidt nodded and intoned, "Well, Principal Stanley, it's quite simple. It is our understanding that you have a girl who is participating in your boys' baseball program."

Principal Stanley nodded and turned toward Coach McCombs, saying, "Wayne, would you like to respond directly to this?"

Coach McCombs said, "Well, it's quite simple. I coach baseball here, and it's my job to put the best team I can on the field, selecting players from our student body." He gestured toward Sky and continued. "Sky Forest is a student here and is more than qualified to be on our baseball team."

Schmidt pounded the podium and thundered, "She's a girl."

Coach McCombs nodded and observed, "Yes, sir, that would seem to be the case. Your point is?"

Schmidt sighed in exasperation and explained, "Our schools sponsor baseball teams for boys.

There are other sports and activities for girls."

The distinguished gentleman next to Matilda stood, looked toward the podium, and said, "Chairman Schmidt, if I may…"

Schmidt stared at him and spat, "And who might you be?"

The gentleman smiled warmly and said, "Thank you for asking. I am Steven J. Maxwell."

One of the school board members across the table asked, "And what standing do you have in this meeting?"

Mr. Maxwell responded, "I represent Matilda and Sky Forest."

Schmidt demanded, "In what capacity?"

Mr. Maxwell paused to look at every member of the school board and then allowed his gaze to settle on Herbert Schmidt. He proclaimed, "I am the former Attorney General of the State of Oklahoma, but now I serve as general counsel to Mr. Wayne Johnstone who is an illustrious alumnus of this school and a prominent investment banker in this community."

Schmidt asked, "How is this any of Mr. Johnstone's business?"

Maxwell answered, "Mr. Johnstone has long been a benefactor of this school and the baseball team. Just recently, he has taken a keen interest in Sky Forest."

Chairman Schmidt challenged, "Sir, I'm not sure that the fact that Mr. Johnstone is a baseball fan gives you any voice in our proceedings."

Mr. Maxwell countered, "Sir, I just recently have agreed to serve as attorney of record for Matilda Forest and Sky Forest. I'm certain neither you, nor this school board, would want to deny them the right to legal representation, particularly as Sky Forest is a minor child."

Schmidt objected. "I'm not sure of the legal precedence here."

Mr. Maxwell interjected, "Well, sir, I am well aware of the legal precedence as I wrote the statutes myself, and presided as Attorney General of the State in drafting the pertinent law."

Schmidt shrugged dismissively and said, "Be that as it may, we still have the matter of a girl who took it upon herself, in clear opposition of our standards, to get involved with the boys' baseball team."

Sky raised her hand and said, "Am I allowed to say something?"

Chairman Schmidt thundered, "No!" but attorney Maxwell stood and proclaimed, "I'm certain that neither the chair nor any members of this school board want to deny a student or her legal guardian the right to be heard in a proceeding that directly impacts them. If you are going to assert such a position, within the hour I will simply file a legal motion that I've already prepared and we will continue this conversation downtown in a more formal setting."

Chairman Schmidt stepped back from the podium as if he had been struck. The other members of the school board fell silent and remained motionless.

After several moments, Schmidt regained his composure, stepped back to the podium, and said, "Sky Forest, if you would like to say something, we will listen to it."

Matilda held Sky's hand to give her encouragement. Sky softly said, "I never thought of joining the baseball team and didn't want to."

Schmidt interrupted. "Then how, pray tell young lady, did you become a member of the Will Rogers High School baseball team who I understand is scheduled to pitch in the opening game next week."

Sky explained, "Well, sir, it all started when you cut the budget, and we lost our softball team."

Schmidt appeared defensive and exclaimed, "You can't mean to say that you're going to sit there and somehow claim I'm responsible for this."

Attorney Maxwell interjected, "I believe that's what she is saying, and it squares with the facts in this case."

Chairman Schmidt stood ramrod straight, adjusted his suit jacket, glanced at his board members, and announced, "Well, sir, the purpose of this emergency meeting of the school board was to determine the facts in this case. I believe the facts are now in evidence, and we have no choice other than to bring this matter to an abrupt conclusion in the following manner."

Schmidt glanced at a file on the podium in front of him, shuffled several papers, and announced, "Unless conditions change before the opening game of the boys' baseball season—specifically referring to having a girl on the team—this board will move to rule that Will Rogers High School will forfeit all their games and the entire baseball season."

Coach McCombs shouted, "You've got to be kidding me!"

Sky burst into tears, and Matilda hugged her.

Steven J. Maxwell, Attorney at Law, thundered, "I object!" but Chairman Herbert Schmidt smiled, closed his file, and stated, "This meeting is over."

Chapter Ten

Point of No Return

*"What constitutes a life well spent,
anyway? Love and admiration from your
fellow men is all that anyone can ask."*
—Will Rogers

10

The school assembly scheduled for that next day was slated to be a pep rally for the baseball team and its upcoming opening game. Coach McCombs called a meeting of the players to be held an hour before the assembly. The players shuffled into the locker room where all of the baseball team meetings were held. They slumped on benches, sprawled on the floor, and leaned against lockers waiting for the coach to explain why they were there.

Coach McCombs emerged from his office and called, "You guys gather around and listen up. We've got some important stuff to go over."

Just then, everyone could hear a timid knock on the locker room door. The coach's impatience and frustration were evident.

He exclaimed, "We're trying to have a meeting here."

The timid knocking persisted, and the door opened a few inches. A halting voice asked, "Can I come in?"

The coach rushed to the locker room door and held it open. He sheepishly said, "Sky, I'm sorry. I didn't think about you when I called the meeting."

Sky shrugged and explained, "Well, I just wanted to be sure all the guys were decent."

Bob Dewitt quipped, "We're not decent, but we're all dressed."

Everyone laughed, and Sky sat on one of the benches. The team directed their attention toward Coach McCombs, and he began, "Guys, I've been a baseball coach for a lot of years and played the game for a lot of years before that, but I've never faced anything quite like this before. A great baseball team plays as a unit. There's no such thing as one player succeeding while the rest fail. I've always believed that there's nothing more important than team unity, shared sacrifice, and sticking together."

The coach paused to glance around the room. Every eye was riveted on him, and he had never heard the locker room so absolutely silent.

He took a deep breath and continued, "There's a guy on the school board who's threatening to shut us down if Sky pitches in the opening game."

Cletus Jefferson asked, "Coach, what does he mean 'shut us down'?"

Coach McCombs sighed heavily and explained, "Clete, the guy says if Sky pitches next week, he will force us to forfeit that game and all the rest of the games for the season."

Michael Fenner asked, "Can he do that?"

The coach shrugged and admitted, "Son, I don't honestly know. I've never dealt with anything like this before."

Sky raised her hand and emotionally said, "Coach McCombs, I've got to speak."

The coach smiled and nodded for Sky to proceed.

She said, "Guys, I really appreciate what the coach, George, and all of you have done, but I can't ask you to risk it. It's too much."

George interjected, "It's our decision, not yours."

Sky shook her head and stated, "No. I can't allow that. They canceled my softball team, which is what got all this started. It was one of the worst things that ever happened in my life. I can't take a chance on doing that to you."

Coach McCombs explained, "Sky, that's not the way we do things around here. I'm in charge of the team, but everybody has a vote on something like this."

Sky responded, "Yes, sir. I understand, but there's something I want everyone to know."

The coach gave her an encouraging nod.

Sky continued, "As most of you know, my folks were killed when I was a little kid and I live with my grandmother. She is a traditional Cherokee Indian, and that's an important part of my life, so I believe in loyalty, honor, and sacrifice. One of my favorite Cherokee sayings is, 'When you were born, you cried and the world rejoiced. Live your life so that when you die, the world cries and *you* rejoice.' Whatever happens here, I want to have no regrets."

Fernando Cruz stated, "Sky, I'm obviously not a Cherokee Indian, but I believe in loyalty, honor, and sacrifice, too."

Cletus Jefferson chimed in. "Well, I'm obviously not a Cherokee Indian either..." Everyone chuckled, and he continued, "...but I believed in what you said about living with no regrets. This is my last year to play baseball here, and I will always regret it if we don't put our best people in the best places to win a state championship."

Cletus pointed his finger directly toward Sky and stared at her, saying, "You are one of the best people, and this is the best place for you. If we don't give this a shot with you on the team, *I'm* going to have regrets."

Michael Fenner agreed, "Here, here."

Coach McCombs took over the meeting, saying, "All right. This is just like a lot of other things we've decided before. Everybody gets a say, and it's got to be unanimous."

The coach reached for his clipboard and read off the names one at a time. "George?"

George smiled at Sky and said, "She plays."

The coach called, "Michael Fenner?"

"She plays," Michael emphatically stated.

The coach nodded and continued. "Fernando?"

He responded, "She's one of us."

The coach read the next name. "Bob Dewitt?"

He quipped, "I think we should have had girls a long time ago."

The coach chuckled and asked, "Ken and Patrick?"

One of the twins said, "We're in."

The coach looked at him and asked, "Which one are you?"

The other twin brother interjected, "He's both of us."

The coach looked at David Allen whose lanky frame was draped over a bench, and asked, "Dave?"

The centerfielder responded, "I'm 100 percent onboard."

The coach looked around the room at some of the backup players and younger guys.

He said, "Show of hands if you're in."

Every hand was raised, and Coach McCombs announced, "It's final."

Sky interrupted, arguing, "Don't I get a vote?"

The coach glanced at her and apologized. "Sorry, Sky. Of course you get a vote."

The room felt silent, and the tension built to a fever pitch.

Sky said to the team, "If I vote yes, we've got to win the state championship."

The locker room resounded with shouts and cheers.

Sky stood and faced the entire team. When everyone was silent, she shrugged and said, "Well, then let's win this thing!"

Coach McCombs concluded the meeting, saying, "You know, as a coach you always hope you'll be proud of your team at the end of the season. I've never been so proud of a team before they even played their first game. Get your uniforms on, and then go over to the assembly and pep rally."

Sky rushed down the hall to the girls' locker room, put on her uniform, and hurried toward the auditorium. She hoped she had done the right thing.

As she passed the statue of Will Rogers, that now-familiar disembodied voice, seemed to say, "It was always my experience that the right thing was never easy, and the easy thing was never right."

Shelley and a handful of her hangers-on were carrying picket signs in front of the school auditorium. The signs read: *Dump Baseball, What's Fair for Girls is Fair for Guys,* and *No Softball Means No Baseball.*

Sky rushed over to Shelley and tried to warn her one last time. "Shelley, I can't give you the details, but you all are really making fools of yourselves. If you could just wait a little..."

Shelly interrupted and angrily waved her sign, saying, "You stand there in your baseball uniform trying to tell us what to do. *You're* the problem!"

Sky shrugged and resignedly stated, "Shelley, I tried."

Inside the auditorium, Sky sat next to George on the front row with all the baseball players.

Principal Stanley walked onstage as the band played "Take Me Out to the Ballgame." Everyone applauded except Shelley and her group who were standing in the back of the auditorium waving their protest signs.

When the applause died down, Principal Stanley said, "In a minute, we're going to introduce and honor our baseball team.

But first, we have a very special announcement. Will Rogers High School has many notable alumni. I would like to introduce three of them right now. Please welcome Wayne Johnstone, William Koslow, and Everett Tally."

The students applauded, and several shouts of "Trio" could be heard.

The three business moguls walked to center stage and glanced at one another. Through their own silent communication they had developed over the past forty years, it was obviously decided that Wayne Johnstone would speak for the group.

He stepped to the podium and began, "On behalf of my former Rogers Ropers teammates and fellow alumni, Mr. Koslow and Mr. Tally, I would first and foremost like to tell you all how excited we are about this year's baseball team. When we played here, we never got to compete for a championship, and we've been following the team for many seasons. While the Ropers have gotten close a few years, Will Rogers High has never won a baseball state championship. I believe, and we believe, that this year can be different."

Thunderous applause broke out in the auditorium. Coach McCombs and all his baseball players cheered and shouted.

When order was restored, Wayne Johnstone continued. "There's one special player who was a last-minute addition to the team who has really made our championship hopes realistic. That, of course, is our own Sky Forest."

An even larger ovation began, and chants of "Sky! Sky! Sky!" grew to a crescendo.

Eventually, Mr. Johnstone was able to continue. "The three of us had an opportunity to spend some time with Sky and her grandmother the other night, and she pointed out an injustice that she wanted to see corrected. So today, I'm proud to say we have raised the necessary funds, and the Will Rogers Ropers softball team will resume practice this afternoon and start their season as scheduled next week."

The crowd went wild. Everyone turned toward the back of the auditorium to look at Shelley and her fellow protestors, but they were nowhere to be seen.

Coach McCombs was introduced and walked to the podium amid cheers and applause.

He began, "I know all of our ballplayers really appreciate your support and enthusiasm. All I can ask of you is to bring that much support and enthusiasm to our opening game next week with the Midtown Lions. Our team has a lot of promise, and I know it will face a great deal of adversity both on and off the baseball field, but I believe they're up to the challenge because I know beyond a shadow of a doubt they will stick together as a team and as a family."

The band began to play the school fight song as streamers fell from the ceiling.

While Sky was nervous and apprehensive about the future, she knew she wouldn't have to face it alone.

Chapter Eleven

IN THE SPOTLIGHT

*"Everybody is rushing to get somewhere, where
they have no business, so they can hurry back
to the place where they should never have left."*
—WILL ROGERS

11

Whether it's Major League baseball, college baseball, or high school baseball, most players, coaches, and fans mark the beginning of springtime as the opening day of baseball season.

It was a gorgeous, sunny day with only a calm and gentle wind. Unlike the turmoil Sky felt as game time approached. It was as if a whole squadron of butterflies were flying in formation in her stomach.

As the last class of the school day ended, Sky and all her baseball teammates headed for the stadium anticipating the first game of the year.

She smiled as she passed the statue of Will Rogers, and she heard the now-familiar voice actually singing, *"Take me out to the ballgame..."*

As Sky approached the stadium, George fell in beside her and exclaimed, "Wow. It's a great day for a baseball game, and I believe our team is ready."

Sky muttered, "The only one on the team I'm worried about is the pitcher."

As they approached the main gate, they could see a mob gathered there including a TV crew, reporters, protesters, cheerleaders, and a lot of fans who were there to offer support and encouragement.

George helped clear the way so he and Sky could get through the gate.

Sky tried to call, "Thank you," to all the fans and "No comment" to all the reporters.

Coach McCombs met Sky and George inside the gate, declaring, "This is the day we've been waiting for."

George nodded and responded, "Absolutely!"

Sky just nodded and hoped she wouldn't be sick.

They were turning to head for the locker rooms when School Board Chairman Herbert Schmidt stepped out of the shadows and thrust a piece of paper toward Coach McCombs, saying, "This is a letter confirming my formal ruling that the Will Rogers High School Ropers baseball team will forfeit the game today and all games for the rest of the season if this girl participates."

Schmidt smiled malevolently and appeared triumphant until Steven J. Maxwell, attorney at law, stepped forward, declaring, "I'm glad you're all here." He thrust a document toward Chairman Schmidt and stated, "This is a court order from the district judge declaring a stay that mandates you take no action regarding Sky Forest participating on the baseball team until the end of the season."

George clapped his hands and said, "I don't know much about it, but I'm guessing a court order from a district judge beats a letter from the school board."

Mr. Maxwell slapped George on the back, saying, "Son, you're absolutely right. Have you ever thought about being an attorney?"

George laughed and replied, "No, sir. I haven't thought much past being a catcher."

Herbert Schmidt's face turned beet red as he looked at the court document. He sputtered, "You haven't heard the end of this," and he stomped away.

Coach McCombs looked at Sky and declared, "Well, it looks like we won."

Sky shrugged and timidly asked, "What will happen at the end of the year?"

Coach McCombs advised, "Worry about today. Let tomorrow take care of itself. Now, let's play some baseball."

Sky found an equipment room under the stadium where she could change into her baseball uniform. Then she joined her teammates in the locker room.

Coach McCombs entered and said, "Okay. Gather 'round and listen up. This is what we've been waiting for and working for, so we've got to make it count. I'd like to turn it over to our captain, George Walters."

George stood, looked at all his teammates, and spoke solemnly. "Guys, it's an honor to get to play with you all. This is my senior year, and several of you are in the same boat with me. This is our last chance to go all the way. I'd like us to dedicate this opening game to Sky, so let's circle up."

All the players gathered in a tight circle and reached a hand into the center. When everyone's hand was touching, George counted, "One, two, three," and the whole team yelled, "To Sky!"

As they went out onto the field for their warmup drills, Sky couldn't believe how many people were already gathered for the game. The stands were filled, fans were lining the fences along both foul lines, and people were still pouring into the stadium. It was like a circus.

Sky felt awkward and disconnected as she tried to loosen up and throw her warmup pitches to George.

He called encouragingly, "Don't worry. Everyone gets a little nervous on opening day. Once you've thrown a couple of pitches, everything will settle down."

The team stood along the first base line and held their hands over their hearts as they sang the National Anthem.

The announcer introduced the players for the visiting team, the Midtown Lions. Sky couldn't help but notice that they all looked big, strong, and fast. Everyone seemed to be staring at her.

Then the voice of the stadium announcer, Adam Hildebrandt, echoed through the public address system. "Welcome to the opening game of the season for the Will Rogers High School Ropers."

A thunderous cheer rose from the stands.

The announcer continued, "And welcome to our visitors, the Midtown Lions."

From the applause and cheers, Sky could tell that a lot of the opposing team's fans had come out for the game. She knew many of them were there to watch her, and she felt as if she were on trial or in some kind of carnival sideshow with people lining up to stare at her.

As each of her teammates were introduced, they stepped forward.

"Now, your starting lineup for the home team. Batting first and playing shortstop, Fernando Cruz. Batting second at third base, Bob Dewitt. Batting third in center field, David Allen. Hitting fourth, batting cleanup, is All-State catcher George Walters."

An enthusiastic roar echoed throughout the stadium. Sky had grown so comfortable with George as her new friend and teammate she had almost forgotten what a great player he was.

When the cheers died down, the introductions continued. "Batting fifth in right field, Patrick Couples. Batting sixth in left field, his twin brother, Ken Couples."

The brothers stepped forward, hugged, and gave each other a high five.

"Batting seventh and playing first base, Cletus Jefferson. Batting eighth at second base, Michael Fenner."

All eyes were on Sky. Cheers and boos reverberated across the field as the announcer concluded, "And batting ninth, and your pitcher for opening day, Sky Forest."

Sky stepped forward next to Michael Fenner. He held out his hand, and she slapped it with far more confidence and enthusiasm than she felt.

Sky took her place on the mound and tossed a few final warmup pitches to George.

Her teammates threw the ball round the infield one last time, and the umpire stepped forward and yelled, "Play ball!"

The first Midtown Lions hitter stepped into the batter's box and pounded the plate with his bat. He seemed formidable and intimidating.

George called to her, "Okay, Sky. Let's fire it right in here."

George pounded his mitt, and Sky wound up and threw the ball. It was about two feet outside, and George was barely able to snag it before it went all the way to the backstop. Jeers and catcalls rose from the Midtown fans.

George threw the ball back to Sky. She tried to calm down and slow her breathing, but her second pitch was outside again, and the umpire yelled, "Ball two."

Sky focused on not letting the ball drift outside and was able to get it right over the plate, but it was too low so she was facing a count of three balls and no strikes on her very first batter.

George placed his catcher's mitt as her target right over the center of the plate, but her pitch feebly bounced in the dirt way outside.

The umpire declared, "Ball four. Take your base."

The Midtown player tossed his bat aside and yelled toward Sky as he was trotting to first base, "Wow. This is going to be easy. I hope you can get at least one pitch in the zone today so I have a chance to swing the bat."

As the runner reached first base, Cletus Jefferson glared at him defiantly and said, "I'd suggest you hold your comments till the end of the game."

The Midtown base runner turned intending to hurl an insult, but Clete's imposing size and intense expression dissuaded him.

Sky stood on the mound as the second batter strode to the plate. She couldn't believe she had walked the very first player she had faced in four straight pitches.

Sky glanced around in panic.

George called, "Time!" and trotted out to the mound.

He said, "Sky, tomorrow's Saturday, and I was wondering if you would go out with me."

She nodded yes, and laughed, saying, "I thought the catcher was supposed to come out here to calm me down."

George shrugged, saying, "Well, I thought it would get your mind off that first batter."

Sky smiled and asked, "So, when you had a guy out here pitching, what did you talk to him about?"

George grinned and answered, "Girls."

The umpire approached, yelling, "Okay, let's break it up and get back to the game."

George took his place behind the plate.

He spoke just loud enough for the new batter to hear. "She still has a little bit of a control problem, but she only hit that one guy, and he's supposed to get out of the hospital next week."

The Midtown batter laughed heartily, but George noticed that he backed up several inches away from the plate.

George set up on the outside edge, and Sky fired one right into his mitt.

The umpire yelled, "Strike one!"

Sky calmed down a bit after getting her first pitch over the plate. She noticed George had set up on the inside edge of the strike zone and was signaling for a curve ball.

She nodded at him, wound up, and let it go. The ball rocketed straight toward the batter's head, but at the last instant, it dove right over the plate, and the umpire called, "Strike two!"

Sky heaved a sigh of relief and noticed George was signaling for her fast ball six inches outside of the strike zone. She wound up and let the pitch go.

The batter lunged at it but hit a feeble grounder between first and second base. Michael Fenner charged, scooped up the ball, and tossed it to Fernando Cruz covering second base. Fernando caught it, stepped on the bag, and fired the ball to Cletus Jefferson on first base. Clete caught it deftly, and the first base umpire signaled *out*. It was a perfectly executed double play.

Sky was relieved that there were two outs and no one left on base as she faced the third batter.

George signaled for a pitch high and inside. Sky delivered it, and it jammed the batter. He hit the ball just a few inches above his hands, and it flew into foul territory.

George threw off his mask and streaked toward the foul ball catching it up against the rail in front of the first row of seats. The home umpire signaled *out,* and Sky felt as if she had dodged a bullet making it through her first inning.

The Ropers struck the ball soundly and got some base runners but failed to score any runs throughout the first few innings. Sky was able to find her familiar form on the mound and got the Lions out without even allowing another base runner through the middle of the game.

Her attempts at the plate were rather anemic. The coach had signaled for her to bunt, but the Lions' third baseman moved so far toward home plate that he was able to throw her out at first base several times and actually caught her bunt in the air once to get her out.

In the seventh inning, the Midtown Lions got several hits, and Sky gave up her first run. The Lions took the lead, one to nothing.

In the eighth inning, George pounded a fast ball over the center field fence tying the score one to one.

Sky got all the Lions out in the top of the ninth inning, and the Will Rogers Ropers came to bat in the bottom of the ninth. With two outs in the inning, Michael Fenner took a walk then stole second base.

The roar of the crowd was deafening as Sky stepped into the batter's box with two outs and the winning run on second base. Once again, the Lions' third baseman crowded toward Sky anticipating another bunt attempt.

He yelled, "This is too easy."

Sky glanced toward her coach on third base, and he was signaling for her not to bunt the ball but to hit away.

Sky took a pitch on the outside edge of the plate, and the umpire called, "Strike one!" Then she fouled off a pitch and realized she was down to her last strike.

The third baseman seemed so close she felt that she could reach out and touch him. He pounded his glove confidently as the Midtown Lions pitcher threw the ball right over the heart of the plate.

Sky swung and connected with the pitch. She hadn't hit it very solidly, but it bounced through the third baseman's legs and rolled into shallow left field. Michael Fenner was off like a shot from second base. The coach on third signaled for Michael to run home. He rounded third and sprinted toward the plate.

The throw from left field bounced into the catcher's waiting mitt but not before Michael Fenner had crossed the plate scoring the winning run.

Chapter Twelve

GOING TO THE SOURCE

"You must judge a man's greatness
by how much he will be missed."
—WILL ROGERS

12

Pandemonium reigned throughout the stadium. Sky was euphoric. Not only had she been the winning pitcher in her first baseball game, she had batted in the game-winning run.

Coach McCombs rushed over, hugged her, and said, "I'm proud of you, but I knew you could do it."

The Trio, dressed in their business suits, approached and each shook Sky's hand and offered their congratulations as if they had just closed a merger deal. Her teammates slapped her on the back and gave her high fives.

Principal Stanley shook Sky's hand and said, "We are all proud of you, Sky."

Several reporters shouted questions at her, and she responded, "I'm proud of our team. My teammates were great. I'm just proud to be a Will Rogers Roper."

Eventually the excitement died down, and Sky saw her grandmother walking toward her.

Matilda said, "Granddaughter, I am very proud of you. You played like an honorable warrior."

Tears filled Sky's eyes as she hugged her grandmother and whispered, "Gram, I'm glad you were here. It wouldn't have been the same without you."

Sky felt giddy as she walked back to the school building to shower and change.

Before she left the locker room, she glanced at herself in the mirror and wondered where her baseball journey might take her.

As she passed Will Rogers' statue, she turned toward him and whispered, "Will Rogers Ropers 2, Midtown Lions 1."

As she turned to go, that voice she was coming to expect said, "The best is yet to come."

George was waiting for her on the sidewalk in front of the school with a smile beaming across his face.

He declared, "You're the best-looking pitcher I've ever seen."

Sky smiled and replied, "I think you're probably biased."

George shook his head emphatically and stated, "Absolutely not, but I'd like to walk you home."

Sky smiled and responded, "Sounds great, George."

They walked in a companionable silence, savoring their victory until Sky asked, "Do you think it's weird I'm feeling this growing connection to Will Rogers? Almost like he's communicating with me."

George shrugged and answered, "Who knows? I think there are a lot more things we don't understand than we do understand, but if you're going to get in touch with someone's wisdom, I guess Will would be a good choice. At least now I know where I'm taking you on our date tomorrow."

Sky turned excitedly and asked, "Where?"

George stated mysteriously, "It's a secret. I'll pick you up at two in the afternoon."

When they reached Sky's house, George hugged her, kissed her on the cheek, and said, "You're the best."

Sky smiled and said, "It was a good game."

George corrected her. "I don't just mean baseball."

Sky stepped onto her front porch and said, "See you tomorrow."

Matilda was waiting for Sky at the front door. She formally stated, "The returning champion is home."

Sky felt as if she were about to burst. She exclaimed, "Gram, it was just awesome. The guys were great. My pitches really worked…" Sky paused and revised her statement. "Well, most of my pitches worked, but I'm going to get better."

Grandmother and granddaughter enjoyed a relaxed, companionable evening reliving every moment of the opening day of baseball season.

Sky lay awake late into the night thinking of baseball games, George, and their date the next afternoon.

She slept in late that Saturday morning, then faced the quandary of what to wear on a mystery date. She finally shrugged and made up her mind that if she didn't know where they were going she would just do her best to be dressed appropriately for whatever the day might bring.

Sky was putting the last touches on her flexible outfit for the mystery date when she heard the doorbell ring.

She called, "Gram, can you get that?"

Matilda opened the front door, smiled, and said, "Good afternoon, George. Welcome to our home. Come in."

George was a bit nervous and stammered, "Thank you, ma'am."

Matilda encouraged George to have a seat and make himself comfortable. He glanced around the living room and was amazed at all the Cherokee decorations and artifacts.

He said, "Mrs. Forest, your home is really beautiful."

Matilda smiled, saying, "Thank you, George."

He asked as he pointed toward a long, ornate stick decorated with beads and feathers, "What is that?"

Matilda glanced over her shoulder and replied, "That is a coup stick. Among Cherokee warriors, any blow or victory against an enemy was considered a coup; but the most valiant act was called 'counting coup,' which involved a warrior touching his enemy with a coup stick and then escaping unharmed."

George responded, "Wow, that's really cool. It's kind of like showing that you could have destroyed your enemy, but not doing it is better than actually destroying him."

Matilda nodded and confirmed, "Yes. Sometimes wars and battles cannot be avoided, but I've always thought the highest calling of any warrior is to be so strong and so prepared that conflict is not even necessary."

George nodded and pointed toward a long, fringed, colorful piece of fabric hanging on the wall.

He asked, "What's that?"

Matilda smiled and spoke with pride. "That's one of my most favorite keepsakes. It is a fancy shawl worn at pow wows. As women dance and spin, the shawls swirl displaying all the beautiful colors and fringe."

George nodded and asked, "What's a pow wow?"

She responded, "It is a Cherokee celebration involving feasting, singing, and dancing."

George was intrigued and said, "I'd like to see that. Do you have to be a Cherokee to go?"

Matilda smiled and said, "No. All are welcome to come, and I would be pleased if you would join Sky and me at the next pow wow."

George replied, "Thank you. That would be really cool."

Sky entered, smiled, and gave George a quick hug. She said, "Hey, George. How's it going?"

He looked at Sky, smiled, and said, "Everything's great, and your grandmother just invited me to go to a pow wow."

Sky mischievously smiled, glanced quickly at her grandmother, and responded to George mockingly, "Oh, did she? Do I get to go? I can't leave her alone for a minute."

They all laughed.

Matilda walked with Sky and George to the front door and said, "You two have a great time."

George nodded and said, "Yes, ma'am, and I'll be looking forward to that pow wow."

As George and Sky walked toward the driveway, George pointed at his mother's battered minivan and said, "I washed it and vacuumed the inside, but it's sure not like The Trio's white stretch limo we went out in last time."

Sky smiled brightly and said, "I think it's perfect."

As George backed the minivan out of the driveway, Sky asked, "So, where are we going?"

George announced, "Well, after you mentioned your sort-of connection to Will Rogers, I decided we would go to the Will Rogers Memorial Museum in Claremore. It's only about a half hour from here."

Sky was excited and enthusiastically exclaimed, "George, that's perfect!"

As they drove out of the city into a more rural area, Sky relaxed, sighed, and observed, "It's really nice to get away from all the reporters, protesters, and even the fans. I think I really needed a day like this."

After Will Rogers' sudden and tragic death in 1935, a groundswell grew across the country and around the world clamoring for a fitting tribute to the fallen hero. A discussion and a debate commenced as to whether a memorial should be built to Will Rogers in California, New York, Oklahoma, or Texas. The final decision was made by Will's widow, Betty Rogers, who felt the perfect site would be the twenty acres near Claremore where she and Will hoped to build their dream home when he retired.

A planning commission was formed to set the course for the Will Rogers Memorial Museum. It included Henry Ford, Elliott Roosevelt, Herbert Hoover, Charles Schwab, and Nelson Rockefeller among other notable figures. People across the country gave nickels, dimes, and quarters during the depth of the Great Depression so there could be a fitting memorial to the life and legacy of the beloved Will Rogers.

A ranch house design by John Duncan Forsythe was selected and built with granite shipped from Vermont and limestone that is native to Oklahoma. A focal point of the memorial became the famous statue of Will Rogers created by Jo Davidson. Ground was broken for the project on April 21, 1938, and the facility was dedicated later that year on November 4, which would have been Will Rogers' 59th birthday. The dedication ceremony was carried coast to coast on live radio and featured a message from President Franklin Roosevelt honoring the life and memory of Will Rogers. Will Rogers, his wife Betty, and three of their children are buried at the site.

George and Sky strolled through the museum's many exhibits featuring paintings, sculptures, and artifacts from Will Rogers' life. George was taken with a display describing Will Rogers being included in the Guinness Book of World Records for an incredible feat of roping skill. Will Rogers threw three ropes at an approaching horse and rider. One lassoed the horse around the neck, one lassoed the rider, and the third caught all four of the horse's legs.

Sky slipped into her jacket as she and George walked out of the museum. They strolled arm in arm toward the actual grave site of Will Rogers. They both fell into a respectful silence.

There was an attractive blonde woman standing in the sunken garden in front of Will Rogers' final resting place. She heard George and Sky approaching, turned toward them, and smiled.

Sky murmured quietly, "Hello."

The blonde woman noticed Sky's jacket with the name *Will Rogers* embroidered on it.

She pointed and said, "I like your jacket."

Sky glanced down and responded, "Thank you. We go to Will Rogers High School."

The blonde woman responded, "That's great. I'm Jennifer Rogers-Etcheverry, Will's great granddaughter."

George said, "I'm George Walters, and this is Sky Forest. It's really incredible to meet one of Will Rogers' family members."

Jennifer replied, "Thank you. I work with the board and staff of the Will Rogers Memorial Museum so I'm here a lot, but I always enjoy coming to this spot and feeling connected to my great grandfather."

Sky hesitated for a moment then spoke. "Recently, I have felt sort of connected to Will Rogers, too. Our history teacher read us one of his quotes about what he wanted written on his gravestone and joking about the fact that he would be sitting there reading it when people came to visit."

Jennifer chuckled softly and said, "He was always saying things like that, and I believe those kinds of deep but humorous statements are what made him famous and influential while remaining very approachable and human."

George and Sky said their goodbyes to Jennifer Rogers-Etcheverry and walked toward the parking lot.

As they were driving away, Sky exclaimed, "Can you believe we actually got to meet her?"

George chuckled and quipped, "It's almost like old Will, himself, had our whole day planned for us."

Chapter Thirteen

ENEMY TERRITORY

"If we only stopped to realize that it is really, after all, the little things that count, why, we would be a wiser and more contented race."
—WILL ROGERS

The following Monday dawned cold and blustery. Sky had been looking forward to the game that afternoon, but she was dreading the fact that the Rogers Ropers would be the visiting team, and they would be playing in the Westside Bears' stadium.

As Sky headed out the front door for school, Matilda hugged her, handed her a lavender envelope with flowing writing on it and said, "I'll be there today cheering for you."

The envelope read, *Mr. George Walters.*

Sky asked, "What's this?"

"It's my invitation for George to join us for the upcoming pow wow."

Sky smiled and jokingly challenged, "Gram, you're going to make me look bad sending him a handwritten invitation."

Matilda smiled knowingly and stated, "Granddaughter, I don't think anyone or anything is going to make you look bad to George Walters."

The school was decorated with posters and banners reading *Beat Westside, Skin the Bears,* and *Go Ropers.*

Sky tried to relax throughout the school day, but she could feel the tension building in her stomach.

As she was walking toward the girls' locker room to pack her things before getting on the bus, Coach McCombs stopped her saying, "Sky, you got a minute?"

Sky smiled and answered, "Yes, sir. As long as I don't miss the bus."

The coach grinned and observed, "I can assure you the bus isn't going to move unless both of us are on it."

Sky looked up at her coach curiously. He took a deep breath, let it out slowly, and said, "Sky, you did a great job during the first game handling the media, the hostile fans, and all the distractions, but today, we won't be on our home field; and I'm afraid that the protests and hostility will be even worse."

Sky nodded and replied, "Yes, sir. I was thinking that would probably be the case."

The coach asked, "Do you know why Jackie Robinson was selected to be the first African American baseball player in the Major Leagues?"

Sky shrugged and answered, "I guess because he was the best ballplayer."

Coach McCombs nodded and explained, "That's part of it, but what really made it possible for Jackie Robinson to break the color barrier was the fact that he had the mental toughness and self-control to take all kinds of attacks and abuse while still keeping his composure."

The coach paused and placed his hand on Sky's shoulder. He asked, "Do you understand what I mean?"

Sky nodded solemnly and said determinably, "Yes, sir, and I'll be ready."

The bus was waiting outside the boys' locker room. Sky hesitated before she boarded as she wasn't sure where all the guys sat and whether or not there was some kind of team protocol.

The bus driver got up from behind the wheel, moved down the three steps to the open door, and said, "Sky, I'm Jim the bus driver for all the road trips."

He offered his hand, and Sky shook it.

He said, "I believe you're sitting on the front row across the aisle from Coach McCombs in the seat next to George Walters."

Jim took Sky's bag and motioned for her to get on the bus. Sky settled into her seat next to George, and Jim handed her bag to her.

George said, "He never carried *my b*ag, but welcome to the Rogers Ropers traveling baseball show."

Sky laughed nervously, reached into her bag, and handed George the lavender envelope.

George was bewildered and asked, "What's this?"

Sky feigned annoyance, saying, "Oh, it's from Gram."

George opened the envelope and looked at the note inside. It read: *Dear George, You are a wonderful young man, and I would be pleased to have you join Sky and me for a trip to Tahlequah for a tour and to enjoy the pow wow. I hope you will be with us on that day and many other days to come. All the best, Matilda Forest.*

George folded the note, put it back into the envelope, and slipped it into his travel bag.

Sky was bursting with curiosity and asked, "Well, what does it say, George?"

He acted as if he were offended and blurted, "You're asking about my personal, private correspondence? I'm shocked!"

Sky elbowed him in the ribs, muttering, "I'll get you back."

Coach McCombs was the last one on the bus. He stood at the top of the steps and looked down the aisle. He glanced at Jim the bus driver, asking, "Everybody on board?"

Jim gave the thumbs up sign, saying, "Yes, sir. All present and accounted for."

The coach addressed the team. "Guys, we want to have fun today and win this game, but we also want to be aware of the fact that there's going to be a lot of hype and hostile people there. Stick together, and always have your teammate's back."

The coach gave a signal to Jim and slid into his seat. Jim closed the door, and the bus rumbled out of the parking lot and away from the friendly confines of Will Rogers High School.

Sky and George exchanged small talk as the bus drove through the city and crossed the Arkansas River into West Tulsa. All of the players seemed tense but exchanged good-natured barbs and insults.

As the bus approached the entrance of Westside High School, Sky was shocked to see TV news trucks and a lot of yelling Bears fans and hostile protesters waving signs saying: *Hang the Ropers, No Girls on the Baseball Field, Will Rogers Go Home,* and *Bears Eat Ropers for Dinner.*

Sky nervously asked George, "Is this normal?"

George glanced out of the window and answered, "I think it is now."

As the bus pulled to a stop in front of the stadium, loud, angry protesters crowded around the bus. The coach stood and called, "Guys, keep your seats for a minute."

Coach McCombs and one of his assistants stepped off the bus amid angry shouts and chants.

The Westside Bears' coach, Steve Stoner, was standing next to the stadium gate. He frowned and coolly shook Coach McCombs' hand saying, "Coach, I can't control all this, and you brought it on yourself."

Coach McCombs shot back, "How do you figure that?"

Coach Stoner replied, "Well, a lot of these folks don't think girls have any business playing ball with the guys—and to be honest, coach, I pretty much agree with them. Is this just some kind of gimmick or publicity stunt?"

Coach McCombs leaned toward his rival, stared directly into his eyes, and stated, "Steve, I've known you a lot of years, and while we haven't really been friends, I've always had respect for you. After you watch our pitcher play today, you can let me know if you think it's a gimmick or a publicity stunt."

Coach McCombs walked back toward the bus and stood at the bottom step. He signaled for Jim to open the door.

David Allen and Cletus Jefferson stepped in front of Sky and paused at the top of the stairs.

Cletus turned toward George and Sky and said, "Me and Dave thought we'd walk into the stadium with you guys."

George glanced out the window at the crowd and simply muttered, "Thanks, Clete."

The mob proved to have more bark than bite, and the whole Will Rogers' baseball team made it safely through the stadium gate.

Bob Dewitt approached George and Sky, saying, "Hey, why don't you guys take a walk out on the diamond before you come to the locker room."

George asked, "What's up, Bob?"

Bob quipped, "George, can you just work with me?"

As George and Sky stepped onto the baseball field, it seemed pristine and picturesque.

Sky observed, "It's really peaceful now, but something tells me in about an hour it won't be like this."

After several minutes, Bob Dewitt stepped through the door that led from the locker room to the visitor's dugout and called, "Okay, guys. We're all set."

George and Sky shrugged and looked at one another in bewilderment.

They stepped into the dugout, and George asked Bob, "So, what's going on here?"

Bob made a calming gesture and implored, "Just trust me."

George glared at him and playfully threatened, "Bob, if this is one of your practical jokes, I'm going to tie you in a knot and make you walk back to school."

Bob intoned, "Oh, ye of little faith."

As George and Sky followed Bob through the door, they noticed in the hallway adjacent to the visitors' locker room that a canvas tent had been erected with a crude sign over the door flap that read, *Sky Forest's Private Traveling Locker Room.*

Sky smiled at Bob and sighed with relief, saying, "Thanks, Bob. I wasn't sure how we were going to handle all that. It's one less thing to worry about today."

Bob Dewitt opened the tent flap to reveal a comfortable space with a canvas chair, a rack to hang clothes on, and a small mirror.

Bob announced, "Now that you've had the full tour, I've been authorized by my teammates to present you with the Sky Forest Away Game Survival Kit."

Sky began to laugh.

Bob reached behind him and handed Sky a headset. He explained, "This is for listening to soothing music as we're walking in and out of the stadium or any other time you don't want to hear all these obnoxious clowns."

Sky beamed and said, "Thank you, Bob."

Bob held up a finger and proclaimed, "But that's not all."

He reached behind him again and presented her with a sign as he explained, "You don't have to say a thing. Just hold this up."

Sky glanced down and read the sign. *No comment. The final score speaks for itself.*

Sky whispered, "Bob, what if we don't win?"

Bob was playfully indignant as he stated, "That, my dear lady, is out of the realm of possibility."

George slapped Bob on the back and quipped, "Dewitt, you're not a total jerk."

Bob responded, "Captain, I'm glad you noticed."

Chapter Fourteen

Into the Fire

*"People's minds are changed through
observation and not through argument."*
—Will Rogers

14

The vile and hateful words that were hurled down from the stands toward Sky as she was taking her warmup pitches stung. She was most worried about her grandmother having to hear such awful things.

Sky was finding it impossible to focus on her pitches until she heard that familiar and calm voice behind her saying, "Don't worry about it. Your grandmother is doing fine."

Sky turned around to look, but no one was there. She gazed up into the stands along the first-base side and noticed her grandmother sitting next to The Trio. As usual, the three men were dressed in their business suits.

Sky smiled as she saw a figure who looked exactly like Will Rogers standing behind her grandmother. He was waving and cheering wildly.

As Sky was taking her last warmup toss, the Westside Bears' coach, Steve Stoner, approached the pitcher's mound and signaled for the umpire. Coach Stoner was red-faced and had his hands on his hips.

The umpire trotted to the mound asking, "What is it, coach?"

The coach pointed his finger at Sky and stated indignantly, "She can't play with her hair like that. It will distract the batters."

Coach McCombs joined the meeting on the pitcher's mound in time to say, "She's not playing yet. She's just warming up."

The Bears' coach stomped his foot, turned without saying a word, and stormed back to his dugout.

The umpire rolled his eyes and turned toward Sky, saying, "I'm certain before the game starts you'll either put that long braid under your hat or down the back of your shirt."

Coach McCombs nodded and confirmed, "Yes, sir. That's exactly what we had in mind."

When everyone was in place, the umpire yelled, "Play ball," and the first Westside Bears' batter strode to the plate.

He yelled at Sky, "Hey, throw one like a girl right over the center of the plate, and I'll hit it over the fence for you."

George signaled for the curve ball. Sky nodded, wound up, and let it fly. The ball seemed to be on a trajectory toward the batter's head. He hit the dirt just in time to see the pitch curve over the plate and hear the umpire yell, "Strike one."

The Bears' coach strode angrily out of his dugout holding a rulebook. He marched directly to the pitcher's mound and, once again, signaled for the umpire. Coach McCombs jogged to the mound to see what was happening.

The Bears' coach yelled at the umpire, "Well, she's not warming up now. The game has started."

The umpire nodded in aggravation and declared, "Yes, coach, the game has started, and you are interrupting it. She has the braid down the back of her shirt, and it's not distracting anyone."

The Bears' coach glanced at the rulebook and explained, "It clearly says any player not wearing the proper equipment while the game is in progress will be ejected."

Coach McCombs sighed in frustration and glared at his counterpart as he said, "Coach Stoner, what are you talking about now?"

The Bears' coach held the rulebook open, pointing to it, and said, "It clearly states all players will wear an athletic supporter during the game."

Coach McCombs blurted, "Oh, come on…"

Sky interrupted as she smiled demurely and turned to her coach, saying, "We're good to go."

Coach McCombs was bewildered and looked at Sky questioningly. She untucked the side of her shirt and discretely rolled down the waistband of her uniform pants to reveal that she was, indeed, wearing a jock strap.

The Bears' coach threw the rule book down onto the mound and stomped on it, shouting, "I can't believe this!"

Sky needled him. "Sir, you can believe it. I find it very handy. I sewed a small pocket in the side, and it's where I keep my keys."

Coach McCombs laughed heartily, and the umpire implored, "Gentlemen, could we please play some baseball here?"

Sky pitched flawlessly through seven innings, and the Rogers Ropers took a two to nothing lead. Then in the bottom of the eighth inning, the Bears got a hit and, with a man on first, Fernando Cruz committed a throwing error on what would have been a routine double play ball. Sky was frustrated and distracted with runners on first and second. She lost her concentration and walked the next batter to load the bases.

The Westside Bears' fans were going wild with the go-ahead run on base and no outs.

Bob Dewitt called time and jogged to the mound to talk to Sky. George joined them.

Bob said, "Sky, keep a close watch on the runner at third base. The second he turns his head, fire the ball to me."

Sky had no idea what was going on, but she nodded and muttered, "Okay."

Bob Dewitt resumed his position standing next to the base runner who was taking a lead off of third base. Bob glanced over his shoulder toward the stands then whispered to the base runner, "Have you ever seen a girl like that?"

The runner glanced away for just a second, but it was long enough for Sky to fire the ball to Bob

Dewitt who caught it and promptly tagged the runner out. Boos reigned down from the stands.

Bob Dewitt yelled to Sky, "Works every time."

Sky laughed and seemed to regain her composure.

The next batter couldn't connect solidly with Sky's fastball, and he dribbled a grounder toward shortstop which Fernando Cruz promptly turned in to a double play, tossing it to Michael Fenner who fired the ball to Clete Jefferson at first a split second before the runner touched the base.

The Ropers took the two to nothing lead into the top of the ninth inning, and it was Sky's turn to bat.

The Bears' coach signaled to his pitcher who promptly threw a fastball that hit Sky in the side.

She fell to the ground and lay motionless. The crowd fell silent. Coach McCombs and the trainer rushed to where Sky had fallen.

The Bears' pitcher approached, saying, "I didn't mean to."

The umpire glared at him and growled, "Son, you go stand on the pitcher's mound."

Matilda rushed out of the stands and ran toward Sky, calling, "Granddaughter. Granddaughter!"

The trainer probed Sky's ribs and said, "Her ribs don't seem to be broken, but she's going to have quite a bruise, and it's going to hurt a lot."

Sky rolled over and saw her grandmother looking at her with tears running down her cheeks.

Sky smiled and said, "Don't worry, Gram. I'm fine."

Coach McCombs turned to the umpire and stated, "We're going to get a substitute."

Sky groaned, stood up, and said through clenched teeth, "No, we're not."

She slowly stumbled toward first base.

The first base umpire looked concerned and asked, "Young lady, are you sure you're okay?"

Sky just nodded determinedly.

Coach McCombs shrugged, looked at the home plate umpire, and said, "That may be the toughest kid I ever saw."

The umpire nodded in agreement, saying, "Me, too."

Fernando Cruz hit a long sacrifice fly that allowed Sky to tag up and move to second base.

Bob Dewitt struck out, then Michael Fenner hit a ground ball to the second baseman. Instead of taking the easy out at first, he threw the ball to the third baseman as Sky was sprinting third. He caught the ball in plenty of time, but Sky managed to slide under his tag and touch third base.

The umpire signaled and called, "Safe!"

The Bears' coach was furious and ran toward his third baseman yelling, "Son, what was that?

Why didn't you tag her out?"

The third baseman sheepishly muttered, "I didn't think she'd slide."

The coach prompted, "Why?"

The third baseman shrugged and replied, "She's a girl."

Coach Steve Stoner pointed at Sky as he glared toward his third baseman, saying, "Son, that's not a girl. That's a baseball player like I wish you were."

He turned and stomped back toward his dugout.

Sky brushed the dirt from her uniform and took a lead off of third base.

George stepped into the batter's box and called to Sky, "Just stand on the base and take it easy. You'll have plenty of time."

The Bears' pitcher threw a fastball over the plate, and George knocked it over the left field wall.

Sky jogged to home plate and waited for George to trot around the bases and join her. George touched home plate, hugged Sky, and asked, "Are you okay?"

Sky nodded and replied, "I think so."

George chuckled and declared, "Anyone who can get hit by a pitch like that then slide into third like you did deserves an easy jog to home plate."

Sky got the first three batters out in the bottom of the ninth, giving the Will Rogers Ropers a five to zero victory. It was her first shutout win.

Her teammates rushed toward Sky to hug her and pat her on the back.

The trainer warned, "Take it easy with her ribs, guys."

He wrapped Sky's ribs causing her to be the last one out of the stadium to catch the bus.

Matilda was waiting for her and looked worried, asking, "Granddaughter, are you all right?"

Sky smiled and cheerily said, "No problem. The trainer just wrapped my ribs to be safe. I was more worried about you sitting in the stands with all those crazy people yelling hateful things."

Matilda nodded and replied, "I didn't even hear them. When people try to say things I choose not to listen to, I go inside myself and repeat words of wisdom."

Sky was bewildered and asked, "Like what?"

Matilda recited a quote from a Cherokee chief, "We are a people who face adversity, survive, adapt, prosper, and excel." Matilda continued, "When you hold thoughts like that inside you and dwell on them, hateful words just seem to drift away harmlessly."

Sky nodded and responded, "Thanks, Gram. I'm going to have to remember that and try it out for myself."

The Will Rogers Ropers' next game was on the road once again, and they won seven to two at the Northtown Cardinals stadium. If anything, the crowd was even more hateful.

After the game, Sky and George were trying to make their way through the hostile fans.

Coach McCombs met them at the bus, saying, "Great game, guys."

Just then, Herbert Schmidt emerged from the angry mob, and pointed his finger at Sky, saying, "This is all your fault. If you'd act like a proper young lady, this wouldn't…"

Steven J. Maxwell, attorney at law, stepped directly in front of Schmidt and held out a legal document declaring, "Chairman Schmidt, this is a duly-executed restraining order requiring you to remain at least five hundred feet away from Sky Forest and her grandmother Matilda Forest until the end of the baseball season when the question you have raised about Sky playing baseball is legally resolved."

Schmidt glared at Sky and Coach McCombs and spat, "Well, how are you going to feel when all of your wins for the whole year are turned into losses?"

Mr. Maxwell signaled to a couple of burly police officers who were positioned a few feet behind him and said, "Mr. Schmidt, these officers are going to assist you in vacating the area and make sure that you maintain the proper distance away from Sky."

As the police officers each took one of Schmidt's arms to lead him away, George quipped, "It looks like two victories in one day."

Chapter Fifteen

GOING TO THE WELL

*"Mothers are the only race of people
that speak the same tongue. A mother in
Manchuria could converse with a mother
in Nebraska and never miss a word."*
—WILL ROGERS

15

The Will Rogers High School Ropers' baseball team seemed unstoppable. They won their next eleven games handily. George Walters was batting .485 and leading the league while Sky's earned run average of 1.52 led all pitchers. Just when Sky was certain nothing could go wrong, something did. She gave up four hits and two walks in the ninth inning, giving the Plainfield Raiders a seven to six victory over the Ropers.

Sky was devastated. She hung her head and trudged toward the dugout.

Coach McCombs patted her on the back and said, "Good game, Sky."

She muttered, "What was good about it?"

The coach chuckled and explained, "Sky, the best teams in the Major Leagues lose a third of their ballgames. Baseball scores are like rainfall."

Sky was bewildered and asked, "What do you mean?"

Coach McCombs stated, "The average annual rainfall in Tulsa is approximately forty inches per year. If we get three or four inches every month, we have a pleasant growth season and an uneventful year. If we get no rain all summer followed by ten inches on one day in the fall, we have a flash flood. What happened to you in the ninth inning today was a flash flood. All the hits and walks came at the same time. If they had gotten a couple of hits or a walk each inning, you would have never noticed it, but it came in a downpour, and we got washed out. There's nothing you can do about it. It's simply the nature of the game."

Sky nodded in understanding, but she was still depressed.

She walked back to the school, took a shower, and put on her street clothes.

As she was exiting the building, a voice from the direction of the Will Rogers' statue said, "Losers don't know how to win, but true winners know how to lose."

George met Sky on the sidewalk outside the school building.

He said, "Cheer up."

Sky said, "I hate to lose."

George chuckled and replied, "I'm leading the league in batting, and I still get out more times than I get a hit."

Sky shrugged and asked, "So, how do you get over it?"

George answered, "Whenever I lose or play a bad game, I try to think about anything I can learn from the experience then leave it behind me and move on."

Sky asked, "How do you do that?"

He explained, "I always try to do something different and get my mind off of baseball. The timing is perfect because I am the proud owner of a handwritten invitation to go with you and your grandmother tomorrow to Tahlequah for a tour and to experience a pow wow."

Sky brightened and exclaimed, "Wow, I'd almost forgotten that's tomorrow."

George just smiled and nodded.

Sky concluded, "We will pick you up early. Gram always likes to make a whole day of it. I think you're in for quite an experience."

George replied, "I have no doubt."

They held hands until they reached Sky's house. George kissed her goodnight, and walked home thinking that it was the best he'd ever felt after losing a game.

Matilda and Sky were up early to prepare a picnic lunch and pack the car. Sky drove as they went to pick up George. When they arrived at his house, Matilda got in the back seat so George could sit in the front with Sky.

Anyone who believes that Oklahoma is a flat and barren land has never been to Tahlequah, Oklahoma, in the Eastern part of the state. The area features the scenic Illinois River, which winds among picturesque and dramatic timber-covered hills.

Matilda offered a travelogue and history lesson from the back seat. "Every time I travel from Tulsa to Tahlequah, I know it takes a little over an hour to get there, but I feel I am transported hundreds of years into our people's past."

George asked, "Mrs. Forest, I know you consider yourself a Cherokee, but do you also think of yourself as an American?"

Matilda responded with certainty, "I do, indeed, consider myself very much an American. The Cherokee people have sacrificed significantly to make this country what it is today. Cherokee fingerprints are all over the landscape of the United States. People are always surprised to learn that American Indians serve in the U.S. military in greater numbers than any ethnic group and have since the Revolution; but we have a checkered past.

"Europeans arrived in North America and thought they had discovered a new world when, in reality, they had discovered a culture that had existed since the Ice Age. They found that Indians in North America spoke more than 300 languages and over 1,000 dialects.

"John Steinbeck, one of my most favorite American authors, said, 'The Indians survived our open intention of wiping them out, and since the tide turned, they have even weathered our good intentions toward them, which can be much more deadly.'"

As they approached Tahlequah, Matilda pointed out various sites and landmarks. Sky took the scenic route so George could get a more full experience. Then she drove them to the Cherokee Heritage Center.

Matilda explained, "Here is where you can get a real feel for our people and our past." She recounted a Cherokee timeline as they walked the grounds. "In 1540, the Cherokees encountered the first European explorers. In 1738, one third of the Cherokee population died in a smallpox epidemic. In 1809, Sequoyah began working on the Cherokee syllabary. And 1838 and 1839 were the years of the ordeal called the Trail of Tears. It was a human tragedy but brought our people to Oklahoma."

Matilda paused and had a faraway expression on her face. After several emotional moments, she continued, "In 1865, the Cherokees offered citizenship to freed slaves; and in 1985, Wilma Mankiller was elected principal chief."

Sky interjected proudly, "She and Gram were friends."

Matilda and Sky showed George the other exhibits at the Heritage Center including the Trail of Tears Exhibit; Diligwa, the 1710 Cherokee village; and Adams Corner Rural Village that features Cherokee history of the late 1890s.

They strolled the grounds and found a quiet spot to enjoy their picnic lunch.

George exclaimed, "Wow! I had no idea. You could spend a week here and not begin to experience everything."

An elderly couple approached and waved excitedly. Matilda exclaimed, "It's my old friends Larry and Mary Lou. I'm going to sit and talk with them awhile and give you kids a break before we go to the pow wow."

Matilda hurried over and hugged her old friends.

Sky explained, "If anybody is more interested in Cherokee history than Gram, it would be Larry and Mary Lou. They love to sit and talk for hours."

George responded, "I'd like to just sit and listen to everything they have to say.

Sky chuckled and said, "That would be great except they're speaking Cherokee."

George was fascinated and asked, "Do a lot of older Cherokees speak the language?"

Sky answered, "Some do, and even some younger Cherokees do as well."

George asked, "You know anyone our age who speaks Cherokee?"

Sky smiled, raised her hand, and announced, "Me."

George blurted, "Sky, I had no idea."

She explained, "Our language is the key to our culture and our past, so it is the foundation of our future. I grew up with Gram speaking our native language to me a lot of the time, so it just came naturally to me; however, it's important to use the language consistently, or you will lose it."

Late in the day, Matilda and Sky took George to his very first pow wow. It was set up as a series of large circles. The center circle was the dance arena, outside of which was the master of ceremonies table, drum groups, and sitting areas for dancers and their families. Surrounding all of that was a larger circle for spectators, and beyond it was an outer circle for vendors offering traditional food, Cherokee artwork, beadwork, leather, regalia, jewelry, and souvenirs as well as music.

The pow wow began with a prayer and the Grand Entry led by the Eagle Staff and flags. Then there were drums and dancers. George had never seen anything like it. The colors, the beat of the drum, and the atmosphere were all mesmerizing.

At the end of the event, George hugged Sky and Matilda, saying, "I want to thank you both for giving me this amazing day and unforgettable experience."

Chapter Sixteen

END OF THE TRAIL

"Popularity is the easiest thing in the world to gain and it is the hardest thing to hold."
—WILL ROGERS

16

The Ropers rolled through the rest of the regular season and breezed into the first round of the state playoffs.

Sky remembered what Coach McCombs had told her about experiencing all the rainfall at once and suffering through a flood. She watched it happen to the Mountain View Bobcats in the first round of the playoffs as Rogers High beat them nine to zero with homeruns from Cletus, George, and David Allen.

That following week at school, Sky saw George coming out of Coach McCombs' office with a handful of letters. She stopped beside him and cheerily asked, "What's up?"

George smiled broadly and explained, "No big deal. It's just today's college mail."

Sky shrugged and asked, "What's college mail?"

George replied, "It's the latest batch of baseball scholarship offers." He flipped through the envelopes, reading the return address labels. "Texas Tech, Florida State, USC, Arizona State, and a whole lot more."

Sky was shocked and asked, "How long has this been going on?"

George shrugged and said, "A couple of months, I guess."

Sky had a sinking feeling. She had never really thought about George going away somewhere to college. The idea of it left her depressed and lonely.

The Rogers Ropers faced the Riverview Ravens in the semifinal game of the state championship. Sky could feel the hype and pressure building with each playoff game.

The tension was broken with some comic relief. After Patrick Couples flied out to right field, the umpire stopped Ken Couples before he could step into the batter's box, challenging, "Didn't you just bat?"

Ken answered, "No, sir, that was my brother."

The umpire muttered, "I'm not going to fall for that. Get your brother out here."

Coach McCombs ran onto the field with Patrick Couples at his side. The umpire stared at the twins then turned to Coach McCombs, asking, "Coach, can you tell these guys apart?"

Coach shook his head and answered, "No. It's always been a mystery to me."

The umpire stepped behind the plate, commanding, "Okay, whichever one of you is up next, let's play ball."

The Ropers scored six runs in the fifth inning, and the game was never in doubt as they rolled to a nine to three victory, putting them in the state championship game the following week against the Metro Capital Cowboys.

When Sky thought about the Metro Capital baseball team, it was a lot like thinking about the St. Louis Cardinals. Metro was a dynasty. Their baseball team seemed to be a permanent fixture in the state championship game each year.

The week leading up to the big game was a blur of interviews, pep rallies, photo sessions, and everybody wanting a piece of Sky's time.

After a grueling day, she told George, "I wish I was just a ballplayer like everyone else."

George answered, "You are a ballplayer like the rest of us, but you're a lot more. The next girl who follows in your footsteps won't have it quite as tough as you do, and someday, it'll just be normal."

Sky felt better. She smiled and said, "Thanks, George. You always seem to know the right thing to say."

The state championship game was scheduled for that next Saturday in Oklahoma City at the Minor League team's stadium. As the Rogers Ropers' team bus arrived, the stadium looked like the Colosseum or Yankee Stadium to a bunch of high school kids.

As they walked toward the locker room, the hallway was lined with photos of all the Major Leaguers who had played Minor League ball in Oklahoma City.

When the team was dressed and ready to go out onto the field, Coach McCombs gathered everyone together and called, "Okay, listen up here."

He glanced toward the locker room door where The Trio were all standing.

Coach McCombs announced, "Guys, as you know, Mr. Johnstone, Mr. Koslow, and Mr. Tally all played their high school baseball at Rogers and have been great fans and supporters of our program ever since. They have a special introduction they want to make."

The three businessmen stepped forward, glanced at one another, and William Koslow spoke. "You all have done something that very few people ever do. You've made it to this championship game, so we wanted you to get a chance to hear from someone who has played in some championships himself."

The team glanced at one another questioningly, but no one had any idea what was coming.

Koslow continued, "George Frazier played baseball at the University of Oklahoma. Then he played ten seasons in the Major Leagues, pitching in two World Series and earning a championship ring when he pitched for the Minnesota Twins."

Koslow paused for a moment, glanced toward the locker room door, then said, "Please welcome George Frazier."

Cheers and applause rang through the locker room.

George Frazier shook hands with Coach McCombs and The Trio and then stood before the team with a beautiful young lady standing beside him.

He said, "Guys, it's great to be here, and since I understand you have a special young lady on your team, I wanted to introduce you to the special young lady on my team. This is my daughter, Georgia, who is currently Miss Oklahoma."

The team applauded, and Bob Dewitt called, "That's what this team needs is more pretty girls hanging around."

Sky glared at him and playfully said, "Shut up, Bob."

Everyone laughed.

Then George Frazier continued. "Guys, I appreciate the opportunity to speak with you for just a few moments before you go out to play in the state championship game. All of us who play this game of baseball are fortunate, and none of us are entitled to get to play baseball much less participate in the state championship. Many players all across the state began their season hoping they could be here today, but you are the fortunate ones.

"I was lucky to get to play in high school, then at the University of Oklahoma, and in the Major Leagues. I got to pitch in the World Series, and a lot of great players never had that opportunity.

"One of the greatest things that baseball gave me was a lot of wonderful friends and great relationships. You will never forget the championship game today, and your teammates in the room here will always be an important part of your life.

"When you go out on the field, make sure you do your best so you represent your school, your families, your teammates, and yourself. Give it your best effort, and leave it all out there on the field today."

The players applauded and were a bit awestruck to be in the presence of a Major Leaguer.

As they filed out onto the field for their warmups, George Frazier singled out Sky, saying, "I wanted to meet you. I'm George Frazier. This is my daughter, Georgia."

Sky shook both of their hands and shyly said, "It's really an honor to meet you both."

She looked at George, saying, "I'd like to ask you how to pitch." Then she turned toward Georgia, saying, "And I'd like to ask you what you do to your hair."

They all laughed.

Then George spoke. "I'll let you and Georgia get together later on the hair, but for now, the best pitching advice I ever got as I was getting ready for the World Series was to be quick but don't hurry."

Sky appeared confused, and George continued. "A game like this makes us all extra nervous, and without realizing it, we get in a hurry. It's especially bad for a pitcher if you rush through your windup or hurry your release. Just relax, and use your natural athletic quickness, but don't hurry or rush anything when you're out on the field."

Sky thanked them both and walked through the dugout and onto the pristine field. It was a gorgeous setting, and there was already a massive crowd on hand for the state championship game.

Legendary sportscaster Chris Lincoln was on the field with a TV crew doing his pregame broadcast. "Hello, everybody. This is Chris Lincoln coming to you from the Oklahoma City stadium for the state championship game between the Will Rogers Ropers and the Metro Capital Cowboys. As you know, the story this week has been about Sky Forest, the first girl to ever play in a state championship game, but even if she wasn't a girl, the story would still be about her pitching against Metro's Ronnie Fletcher. It sets up to be a classic pitcher's duel today between the finesse of Sky Forest and the power of six-foot-five, 240-pound Ronnie Fletcher who you may have heard has already been drafted by the Kansas City Royals.

"You know, if this was a seven-game series, you'd have to favor the balanced attack of Rogers, but given that it's only a one-game championship, it's going to be hard to beat the power of Metro.

"Another factor today will be the stress and nerves. Metro has played in this kind of atmosphere for many years, but it's a first for the Will Rogers' kids."

Metro was the home team because of their undefeated record, so Will Rogers batted first.

Fernando Cruz stepped into the batter's box, and Ronnie Fletcher threw the first pitch of the championship game. It was like a bullet. Fernando swung but was too slow, so his swing was late. Fernando took a called strike two then struck out as he swung behind another blazing fast ball.

As he stepped back into the dugout, he proclaimed, "That guy is awesome. I can't even begin to get the bat around on him."

Coach McCombs encouraged the team. "Don't panic. Just watch his motion, and start your swing a little earlier."

As predicted, it turned into a battle between the two pitchers. Sky's curve balls nicked the corner of the plate, and Metro batters couldn't hit her pitches any better than the Ropers were doing with Fletcher's powerful fastballs.

The game was scoreless going into the ninth inning when George knocked a single over the second baseman's head. The Ropers' dugout came to life with excitement having a runner on base in the ninth inning, but their hopes were dashed when the next batter struck out to end the inning.

Metro came to bat in the bottom of the ninth needing only one run to win the state championship.

The first batter hit a ground ball toward shortstop that Fernando scooped up and fired to Cletus at first base for out number one. Sky used her sinking curve to strike out the second batter, leaving the Rogers Ropers needing only one more out to send the state championship game into extra innings.

George gave the signal for a fast ball on the outside corner. Sky wound up and threw the ball.

The crack of the bat that echoed throughout the stadium broke Sky's heart. She knew she had given up the winning run to the Metro Capital Cowboys with two outs in the bottom of the ninth inning. The ball soared into the night sky dramatically lit by the bright stadium lights.

Sky lowered her head in defeat, but then out of the corner of her eye, she spotted a blur racing toward the centerfield wall. It was David Allen running faster than she had ever imagined he could, stretching his improbably-long legs to their limit. He raced across the warning track without slowing down, then ran two steps up the vertical wall and leapt incredibly high as he stretched out his six-foot-six-inch frame to its limit. Then he crashed onto the top of the wall, rolled off of it, and plummeted down onto the field.

A hush fell over the stadium. Sky's thoughts of losing the state championship were washed away in an instant by worries about her teammate lying motionless on the warning track at the base of the centerfield wall.

She sprinted toward David Allen and was joined by George, Coach McCombs, and the trainer as they all rushed toward their fallen teammate. Sky kneeled down beside David, and George looked over her shoulder. David Allen was unconscious.

The trainer waved for the ambulance crew to come on the field and yelled for them to bring the backboard.

Coach McCombs noticed that the umpire had joined them.

He said, "Coach, take all the time you need. We're all praying for your boy there."

Sky began to cry softly. George put his hand on her shoulder to comfort her.

David Allen opened one eye and weakly mumbled, "Haven't you heard there's no crying in baseball? I believe this is yours." He opened his glove to reveal the baseball nestled in the pocket.

The umpire raised his arm into the air with his thumb extended and called, "You're out!"

The ambulance crew eased David Allen onto a backboard and strapped him down.

Sky heard one of them say to the other, "We've got to be careful with the neck and back to try to minimize paralysis."

They loaded David onto a stretcher and rushed him to the waiting ambulance. The fading sound of the siren was mournful and hopeless.

The mood was somber in the Ropers' dugout.

Coach McCombs said, "Guys, I know we're all worried about David, but we're going into extra innings, and we've got to bear down and try to focus."

George glanced at the coach and asked, "Can I say something?"

Coach McCombs nodded and motioned, stating, "Son, it's all yours."

George's voice shook as he said, "We've got to win this championship...for Dave."

The players yelled and clapped.

George called, "Everybody put a hand in."

The team formed the circle with all of their hands touching in the center.

George said, "For Dave." Then counted, "One, two, three."

The team yelled in unison, "For Dave!"

Ken Couples was up first for the Ropers in the tenth inning. He hit a sharp line drive, but Metro's right fielder caught it for the first out.

The Will Rogers' fans sprang to their feet as Cletus Jefferson hit a double to left field.

Michael Fenner came up to bat with one out and the potential winning run on second base. He slapped a ground ball between first and second. Metro's second baseman snagged the ball and tossed it to their first baseman a split second before Michael got there. There were now two outs, but Cletus Jefferson had made it safely to third base on the play.

Sky got her bat and walked toward the plate. The now-familiar scornful jeers and mocking insults resonated across the field. Sky glanced at Cletus on third base. He gave her a confident smile and flashed the thumbs-up signal.

Coach McCombs gave the sign for the squeeze play that required Sky to bunt toward first base allowing Cletus to run to home plate.

Sky thought about David Allen strapped to a backboard in the back of an ambulance racing toward the hospital. She thought about everything she had gone through since that fateful day they had eliminated her softball team. She thought about George and all the guys in the dugout.

She glanced across the plate at the opposite batter's box which should have been empty, but Will Rogers appeared to be standing there. He chuckled, scratched his head, and said, "The key to life is knowin' what's best, then doin' your best."

The legendary figure seemed to fade into mist as Metro's pitcher, Ronnie Fletcher, threw a blazing fastball toward the outside corner. Sky leaned forward and got her bat in front of it. The ball trickled down the first base line as Cletus Jefferson thundered toward the plate. Metro's first baseman gloved the ball and tossed it to the catcher who was poised to tag out the base runner.

As the catcher caught the ball, Cletus slid toward home plate. A cloud of dust rose into the air, and Sky's heart stopped until she heard the umpire yell, "Safe!"

The next batter struck out, but Will Rogers High had the lead.

The Ropers all hugged one another in celebration, and George called, "Okay, let's get these guys out, and the championship is ours."

Sky added, "And David's."

Sky managed to strike out the first Metro batter in the bottom of the tenth inning. The second Metro batter hit a foul ball near the first base dugout. George was able to catch it just before it went into the stands. Sky faced the next batter with two outs and no one on base.

After throwing a ball and a strike, George gave the signal for Sky's curve ball. The batter hit a wicked line drive directly at Sky. She threw up her glove to protect her face and somehow caught the ball.

Sky was trying to catch her breath as George rushed to the mound and hugged her.

She admitted, "I wasn't even trying to catch it. I just wanted to protect my face."

George lifted her off the ground, laughed heartily, and said, "That's great because I like your face just the way it is…and we're the state champions!"

Chapter Seventeen

A NEW PATH

"No man is great if he thinks he is....
All there is to success is satisfaction."
—WILL ROGERS

17

The Ropers' fans were euphoric, and the Metro fans sat in stunned silence.

Sky and George joined in the team's celebration and answered questions for a couple of quick interviews but then hurried to shower and get dressed.

They met outside the stadium and noticed Matilda standing near the bus talking to Coach McCombs. Sky hugged her grandmother, and they shared a special moment.

George asked, "Coach McCombs, is it okay if Sky and I go with Mrs. Forest to check on Dave in the hospital and then ride back to Tulsa in her car?"

The coach nodded and said, "Tell David we're all praying for him, and I will see him just as soon as I can get done here."

Sky drove her grandmother's car through the unfamiliar streets of Oklahoma City. Thanks to George's smart phone, they found the hospital quickly.

Matilda said, "Sky, just pull up to the main entrance, and you and George can go on in to see your friend. I'll park the car and meet you in the waiting room."

Sky and George rushed into David Allen's room. A doctor was shining a light in David's eyes and checking his reflexes. He turned at the sound of the door opening.

He looked at George and Sky and said, "This is a restricted area. It's for family members only."

David Allen said, "Doc, they're family."

The doctor nodded and continued to examine David.

George asked, "Doctor, how is he?"

The doctor jotted several notes in the chart and then turned toward George and Sky, answering, "This young man is very lucky. He's going to be sore for a while and have to do some physical therapy, but I expect a full recovery."

Sky sighed and said, "Thank you, doctor. That is great news."

The doctor winked at Sky and smiled, saying, "You pitched an amazing game tonight. I saw it on the TV in the doctor's lounge earlier this evening."

Sky's face reddened and she stammered, "Well, we just wanted to check on him."

The doctor chuckled, shook George's and Sky's hands, and declared, "It's amazing to have a great pitcher, a great catcher, and a great centerfielder all in the same family."

The doctor left the room, and Sky moved to David's bedside, reached into her bag, and handed him the baseball, saying, "I know you were kind enough to return this ball to me, but I thought you should have it."

David held the ball and noticed she had signed it. It read, *To David, a state champion. Thanks, Sky Forest.*

Coach McCombs rushed into the room, asking, "David, how are you?"

David shook the coach's hand and said, "Coach, they say I'm going to be a hundred percent, but I've got to be honest with you, after tonight, I don't think I ever want to play baseball for you again."

The coach looked shocked but then smiled, saying, "That was the last game of the season for your senior year. You can't play for me anyway."

David shrugged and said, "My decision is final."

Everyone laughed and enjoyed the fact that David would fully recover, and they were all champions.

The banquet to celebrate the baseball season and the state championship was two weeks after the big game. It was held at Tulsa's historic Mayo Hotel, which Will Rogers had visited many times.

Everyone was excited that David Allen was able to join them for the special evening. He was still in a wheelchair and wearing a neck brace, but just having him at the banquet lifted all of their spirits.

After everyone enjoyed a delicious dinner, Principal Stanley walked toward the podium.

Herbert Schmidt blocked his way and said, "Principal Stanley, as the chairman of the school board, I demand to speak to everyone here and render my final decision requiring Will Rogers High School to forfeit all their games for this season and relinquish the state championship."

Principal Stanley responded, "Mr. Schmidt, I have one speaker on the agenda first. Then I will turn it over to you."

The principal stepped to the podium, welcomed everyone, and congratulated them on a monumental baseball season. He announced, "Ladies and gentlemen, we have several requests from elected officials to speak to you tonight. So first, I would like to recognize and welcome the governor of the great state of Oklahoma!"

The governor waved and smiled as the crowd applauded enthusiastically.

He stood behind the podium and spoke with the ease of an experienced politician. "Ladies and gentlemen, I want to congratulate you on winning the Oklahoma State Baseball Championship. Metro Capital won it for so many years in a row. It's kind of nice for me to get out of Oklahoma City and get over here to visit you all in Tulsa."

Enthusiastic applause sounded throughout the ballroom.

The governor continued, "This baseball season has been special for Rogers High School for a lot of reasons including Sky Forest."

A rousing ovation followed the mention of Sky's name.

The governor continued, "I realize there are a few sad souls who don't share your enthusiasm for girls who want to participate in all school activities; therefore, with the help of the former Attorney General of Oklahoma, Mr. Steven J. Maxwell...," the governor paused to nod toward Mr. Maxwell, "...I am proud to announce tonight that we introduced a bill in the Oklahoma legislature that passed unanimously, and I had the privilege of signing it into law this morning."

The governor reached into his jacket pocket, took out a sheaf of papers, and unfolded them on the podium. He slipped on his reading glasses and read, "The Sky Forest Equal Participation Law calls for every student in the State of Oklahoma to have equal access to all school activities for which they are qualified regardless of gender."

The crowd rose to their feet as one and applauded wildly.

Principal Stanley shook hands with the governor and thanked him for coming. The governor waved to the crowd as he and his aides walked out of the ballroom.

Principal Stanley said, "And now I would like to recognize School Board Chairman Herbert Schmidt who wanted to make an announcement."

An anemic smattering of applause quickly died out. An awkward silence ensued as everyone looked around the ballroom.

Finally, Principal Stanley stepped to the podium, shrugged, and said, "Well, it appears that Mr. Schmidt doesn't have an announcement to make after all."

Everyone applauded enthusiastically.

Coach McCombs gave out a number of awards building up to the top honor.

He announced, "And now, I would like you to welcome our Most Valuable Player selected by our team. Please welcome Sky Forest."

Sky was stunned. She tried to compose herself as she made her way to the podium. Coach McCombs hugged her and handed her the ornate Most Valuable Player trophy. He motioned for her to step up to the microphone.

As the applause dwindled into silence, Sky spoke, "I want to thank you guys for picking me, but there are a lot of people I have to share this honor with. First, I have to thank my grandmother. She has been both Mom and Dad to me and has always encouraged me to be everything I could be and a little bit more. I want to thank Coach McCombs and his staff for giving me a chance and my fellow teammates for accepting me as one of the guys. Finally, I have to thank George Walters who believed in me more than I believed in myself."

Sky held the trophy up and proclaimed, "Together, we are all champions."

It was a magical evening Sky knew she would never forget.

The next week as George and Sky were walking down the school hallway holding hands, a gentleman approached and stated, "I wanted to introduce myself. I'm the head baseball coach at Rogers State University, and I would like to make you an offer."

Sky moved away so George could speak with the coach.

The coach turned toward her and asked, "Well, aren't you at least going to listen to what I have to say?"

Sky stammered, "I'm sorry, sir. I thought you wanted to talk to George."

The coach smiled broadly, declaring, "I do want to talk to George, but what's a great catcher without a great pitcher?"

Sky admitted, "Sir, I wasn't really planning on playing baseball anymore."

The coach shot back, "Why not?"

Sky said, "Well, I'm a girl..."

The coach interrupted. "I may be just an old baseball coach, but I can tell you're a girl. I can also tell that you're a great pitcher, and I want you on our team."

George said, "Coach, tell us a little about the university."

The coach handed each of them some literature and said, "Rogers State University offers a wide range of four-year degrees in field such as business, nursing, communications, and many others. Our Center for Studies-at-Large allows our students to learn about other cultures, customs, and locations through programs in the United States and abroad. We have a beautiful campus that includes a 120-acre nature conservancy, and we are located next to the Will Rogers Memorial Museum."

George and Sky smiled and looked at one another.

The coach asked, "Do you know where that is?"

George nodded and answered, "Yes, sir. We've been there."

They all agreed to resume the discussions at the Rogers State University campus the following day.

George, Sky, and Matilda drove to Claremore the next morning and enjoyed a very impressive tour of the Rogers State University campus.

Sky turned to George and said, "This is perfect for me because I can be close to Gram, and they have everything here I could possibly want, but you can get a full scholarship to go to college almost anywhere in the country."

George looked at Sky and declared, "I think everything that I want is right here."

Matilda enjoyed some of the university's exhibits as George and Sky walked across the campus.

George said, "I can't think of any reason we wouldn't do this. They're offering us both a full scholarship."

Sky nodded and said, "George, I just don't want you to regret staying here with me instead of going to one of the big, prestigious schools."

George held her hand and declared, "Sky, I don't think I'll ever regret being with you."

They kissed, and Sky heard a voice coming from the trees along the campus fence line that said, "Well, it looks like we're going to be neighbors."

About the Author

In spite of blindness, Jim Stovall has been a National Olympic weightlifting champion, a successful investment broker, the President of the Emmy Award-winning Narrative Television Network, and a highly sought-after author and platform speaker. He is the author of forty books, including the bestseller, *The Ultimate Gift,* which is now a major motion picture from 20th Century Fox starring James Garner and Abigail Breslin. Eight of his other novels have also been made into movies with two more in production.

Steve Forbes, president and CEO of *Forbes* magazine, says, "Jim Stovall is one of the most extraordinary men of our era."

For his work in making television accessible to our nation's 13 million blind and visually impaired people, The President's Committee on Equal Opportunity selected Jim Stovall as the Entrepreneur of the Year. Jim Stovall has been featured in *The Wall Street Journal, Forbes* magazine, *USA Today,* and has been seen on *Good Morning America, CNN, a*nd *CBS Evening News. H*e was also chosen as the International Humanitarian of the Year, joining Jimmy Carter, Nancy Reagan, and Mother Teresa as recipients of this honor.

Jim Stovall can be reached at 918-627-1000 or Jim@JimStovall.com.

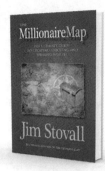